MW01179138

EARTH ALIENS

The Time of Trying Souls

S.E. Wendel

EPIC
Press

The Time of Trying Souls
Earth Aliens: Book #3

Written by S.E. Wendel

Copyright © 2016 by Abdo Consulting Group, Inc.

Published by EPIC Press™
PO Box 398166
Minneapolis, MN 55439

Cover design by Dorothy Toth
Images for cover art obtained from iStockPhoto.com
Edited by Clete Barrett Smith

LIBRARY OF CONGRESS CATALOGING-IN-PUBLICATION DATA

Wendel, S.E.
The time of trying souls / S.E. Wendel.
p. cm. — (Earth aliens ; #3)
Summary: The human colony celebrates it first year on their new home planet, while
still being at odds with the native population. However, the leader of the Charneki,
Zeneba, has many reasons to not trust the new inhabitants.
ISBN 978-1-68076-024-8 (hardcover)
1. Aliens—Fiction. 2. Human-alien encounters—Fiction. 3. Extraterrestrial
beings—Fiction. 4. Science fiction. 5. Young adult fiction. I. Title.
[Fic]—dc23
2015935813

EPIC
Press

EPICPRESS.COM

To Kayla and Jolie, my platonic soulmates

I

The wrench snapped in half, and Hugh O'Callahan went flying back, a piece still in his hand. His palm stung from the force of the break, and he felt content to lie there and give up on the whole thing.

Mikhail Saranov, the head engineer, leaned over him with a sympathetic smile.

"Getting the best of you, is it?"

"This damn thing won't budge," Hugh grumbled, sitting up.

"Oh c'mon now," Saranov said, waving a hand at him.

He strode over to the cable and its rigging and

gave it a good long look. They had been down there all night, in the mines. Over a year on their new planet—longer than they were used to, totaling 524 days—and still they were having trouble getting the mining operation going.

It had been discovered by a science expedition that the tundra region they now called home was strewn with blue rocks, which they were calling cerulean, that had a composition similar to coal. In short, it could be used as fuel.

It was good news for them, the 40,000 lucky lottery winners who had boarded great starships and made the impossibly long journey as the vanguard of an attempt to remove humans from Earth and start anew. Their colony, New Haven, relied on generators converted from the starships' engines, but it was too far north to grow much. Farmland forty miles south had been found suitable, and three hundred people had been allocated for farming and guarding. However, since power lines were out of the question—too dangerous, exposed to both the elements and the natives—cerulean fuel became the next best source of power for the farming operation. That was, if they could actually harvest any of the cerulean.

Their attempts thus far had met with one disaster after another. They had soon learned that the cerulean could not be mined like substances on Earth; if handled too roughly, the stones disintegrated into powder, which did not burn nearly as well as the solid. This coupled with mismanagement and opposition to make the mining outfit a painful failure in the making, which inevitably endangered the farming colony.

There were some who did not want to use the mine, recalling that it had been won by bloodshed. The humans had quickly discovered their new home was already populated by an intelligent species, one who resisted human colonization. It was their mine the humans used. The mine stood next to an abandoned village, a stark reminder of the damage already done by the humans.

Hugh sat up straight and gathered his legs in front of him, watching, rather satisfied, as Saranov tried his hand, and wrench, at the bolt. The engineer's face turned dangerously red as he tried every which way to loosen the jammed bolt.

"Told you," Hugh said as Saranov took a step back and wiped his forehead.

"That's in there."

When they had gotten to the mine to inspect the latest damage, they found many of the cogs, bolts, and cables covered in an almost-solidified sticky substance. It had taken three days to find a solvent for the compound, and by that time it had seeped into everything, acting virtually like glue.

No one was saying it, but Hugh thought the cause was obvious: sabotage.

Though they had been pushed back to their city to the southwest, natives were still spotted now and again in small bands. The nearest of their settlements was 150 miles to the east, and their large city was 400; because of this, the natives sighted were thought to be scouting parties.

The military suffered none of it. The attack on the mine that had left half the equipment covered in solidified sludge hadn't gone unpunished. Word was that a squad had gotten into a skirmish with a native party and had actually captured one, despite the natives being good at slipping away, back into the terrain they knew so well. That was the gossip at least; there was still no official word from the general's headquarters.

Not that there necessarily would be. General Hammond, the self-proclaimed leader of the colony, had seized what amounted to absolute control. There had been no elections, as was previously promised—everything came from her headquarters, which was growing increasingly silent. Civilians were rarely informed, and now even Hugh and Saranov, whose department was technically under the military, were going without news.

"Well we're certainly not getting this running by tomorrow," Saranov said, stretching out his back.

"The general did want it fixed as soon as possible," Hugh reminded him. He wasn't, however, inclined to get up again.

"If she wants to come down and get these things unscrewed, then by all means. Until then, we keep applying solvent and praying."

Hugh couldn't argue with that. He took the hand Saranov offered him and creakily stood up. Everything was sore.

Light seeped down into the mine from the great mouth above. When Hugh looked up, he saw the first shift of miners coming down the stone steps carved into the cave wall. They would be disappointed to hear it was to be another day of digging the old fashioned way.

Once the miners had gotten down and were informed that the equipment still wasn't fixed, Hugh, Saranov, and the rest of the team headed up into the misty morning.

It was autumn again and the ground was beginning to freeze at night. No one looked forward to winter, though there was the silver lining that winter nights were only about as long as a summer night back on Earth. The reason for this was that Terra Nova orbited a star that was in a binary system. During the warmer seasons, the days were long, the nights short, and the temperature similar to an Earth summer, even though the planet was further from its suns than Earth had been. Beginning in autumn and during winter, the second sun was hidden behind the other and things got much cooler as a result.

Hopping into the back of a cruiser, the team drove the seven miles back to New Haven. The path was now well-worn, with all manner of foot and vehicle traffic heading to and from the mine. Many trees, impossibly large as they were, had been felled to make the road relatively straight.

Hugh longed to go to sleep yet had no desire to be home. It was painfully quiet there.

Saranov gave him a thump on the back. Hugh tried to smile. The cruiser eased to a stop on the outskirts of the military's section of the residential quadrant.

The colony was growing quite expansive, now taking up about three square miles. It was sectioned off into four quadrants: military, industrial, market, and residential. Only those with clearance got into the military quadrant, and industrial also had limited access, requiring a work ID. The market had all manner of buildings: shops, schools, warehouses—basically anything that hadn't qualified in any of the other three. Many civilians, those colonists who had been put to cryogenic sleep for the seven-year journey, held jobs there. The residential quadrant was perhaps the largest, rivaled only by industrial. Everyone lived there, though military personnel were grouped together. Hugh's apartment was on the outskirts of this group.

It was beginning to look much homier in the colony, with native plants growing again in open patches of dirt. During construction, the ground New Haven was built upon was levelled, all the shrubs and grass, and most of the trees, uprooted to make room for buildings. Now that they were established, plants grew again. There was a little sapling outside Hugh's apartment building.

He trudged up to the second floor and walked down the hall to door 256. Holding his hand against the cold scanner, the glass panel blinked bright green, and the door unlocked with a *click*.

The apartment was cold and dark, doing little to shake his melancholy. He went straight for the small kitchen, deciding to cut himself a small piece of bread. It would be his last one before winter. Despite the farming colony's precariousness, they had managed to grow some crops during the warmer months, and had brought in sufficient amounts of grain to put in storage and even make bread. The winter promised a subsistence on oats and protein packs.

He heard a small noise and turned. Sitting at

the small wood table, one of the few adornments of the living room, was his brother, Rhys. Hugh swallowed the hunk of bread in his mouth, and it went down dry.

Back on Earth, he and Rhys had been twins and inseparable. Boarding the starships when they were eleven, they had been split up; Rhys was sent to the Cryo Bay and Hugh to an apprenticeship under Saranov. The seven-year journey didn't affect Rhys, and he woke still an eleven-year-old, whereas Hugh was eighteen. Now, almost thirteen and twenty, nobody took them for twins.

"Morning," Hugh said.

Rhys continued to chew his cooked oats, refusing to look at Hugh.

Hugh hadn't expected a response and tried not to be hurt from not getting one. It stung nonetheless, no matter how numb he thought he was to Rhys's silence.

His brother had barely spoken to him the past year. It had been rough for Rhys when he first woke up, finding he had an older brother rather than a twin. The transition hadn't gone well from the beginning. Things deteriorated, Hugh seeing now that trying to make Rhys follow in his footsteps as an engineer was a mistake.

This was not altogether why Rhys remained cold. Hugh hated to recall the night of the attack, when the humans stopped the natives from reclaiming the mine. Rhys had jumped the perimeter right before, and Hugh went after him. When he saw natives attacking Rhys, he hadn't thought, just shot at them and grabbed his brother. He hadn't touched a gun since.

He had hit at least one of them, he thought the smaller one, which had bought him enough time to drag Rhys back to New Haven, though that had been a struggle in of itself. It was only after they got back to New Haven that it sunk in. He killed someone. He was never rid of that ache.

Rhys never spoke of that day, but Hugh finally guessed what Rhys had been doing all those times he jumped the perimeter: he had befriended one of the natives. Rhys was no friend of the regime, especially now, and even before the attack had sympathized with the natives.

Hugh knew he had done wrong. He tried not to think about it, but every night he heard the cries of the natives and Rhys wailing beside him. While trying to protect him, he had made himself Rhys's enemy.

Gulping down a glass of water, Hugh continued to stand in the kitchen. Most of the time he didn't see Rhys when he came home, as he went to bed before he even got up. Hugh slept during the day, working mostly with Saranov at night. Rhys had school, when he felt like attending, and a job at one of the small food shops in the market quadrant. Now on this rare occasion, Hugh was rooted in place, wondering what to say.

He was spared the anxiety as Rhys wolfed down the rest of his oats, dropped the bowl in the sink, grabbed his jacket, and was gone from the apartment.

The slam of the door echoed in Hugh's ears as he slumped down at the dining table. Putting his head in his hands, he almost couldn't believe two of them lived in the apartment. Hugh knew Rhys preferred it this way. That didn't make it hurt any less.

———————

The sky was streaked with orange and red as Nahara, with Undin half hidden behind her, began mounting the horizon. The sunlight hit Zeneba, leader, *mara*, of the Charneki, but it did not warm her. She had quite forgotten the sensation.

She drew her arms and gray robe around herself as she neared the tomb. It was a great rectangular monument, made of solid jade which glistened in the morning light. On the top was carved a figure in repose, his eyes closed, his body covered in a shroud. Within the stone rested her brother, Zaynab.

She could hardly bear to look upon the tomb, but she forced herself anyway. It filled her with hate, and hate was the only thing that kept her alive.

Zaynab had been murdered by a demon. He had come with her to the north, to try and see if they could reclaim the lost territory, and she had no one to blame but herself for that mistake. He should not have come. She should not have let him.

The hatred she reserved for herself made her want to throw herself off the highest turret of Karak so that she might join her brother. Yet that which she bore for the demons made her want to persevere, if only for vengeance.

She heard the quiet tread of footsteps coming up behind her and, from reflex, went to wipe her tears, but she found none. Her eyes had long since dried up, and all that was left seemed dust.

"What is it?" she said, her voice low and missing its former lilt.

"They ask for you."

It was Ondra, her childhood friend from the mountains who had followed her to Karak. He was determined to make a warrior of himself, and she had seen to his being admitted to her personal Guard. A cycle ago she had sent him north with a scouting party to try and discover all he could about the demons.

She hadn't sent him north again. Not since Zaynab's death. She didn't think she could bear it. Yet whenever he was near, whenever anyone she cared about tried to come close, it also pained her. They thought she couldn't see the way they looked at her, full of pity and pain, but she did, and it made her chest feel hollow.

"What do they want this time?" she asked.

"The outfit is back—they wish to report to you."

"Either they did what I ordered or not." She looked at him over her shoulder. "Which is it?"

Ondra linked his hands behind his back and

gazed at her with measured eyes. She could see the pain he tried to hide.

"You should hear what they have to say."

She resumed looking at the dawn. "So, it went badly."

"I didn't say that."

Sighing, she turned to him. "Leave me be, Ondra."

He shifted but didn't withdraw.

"Please, Zeneba, I can't make another excuse, not again. You must come with me."

Her face darkened with a frown, and she refused to look at him anymore. She heard his true wish as if he had voiced it; he wanted her to take her throne back from her council. She had handed it over before travelling north and had yet to offi-cially reclaim it.

"I don't much feel like being *mara* today."

"You haven't been *mara* since he died."

She turned on him, her eyes fierce and pained, but he didn't shrink back. He watched her, and she realized he was trying to barb her, to get anything at all from her.

Straightening, she composed herself, letting the numb wash over her again.

"Very well then."

He bowed to her as she walked past him then followed her towards the Red Hall, the topmost point of their mountain-city.

The Hall fell to a hush when she entered. Her council, mostly comprised of turquoise-robed Elders, stood about the room, encircling a small group of warriors standing before her seat. They all parted quickly for her as she walked up to the dais.

She met Elder Vasya's stony glare. The Elder, once her tutor and head councilor, had become her greatest critic, even travelling with her north to continue his naysaying. In her absence, he had been elected the head councilor once more and stood next to the red seat. She would have preferred to hand the office to Elder Zhora, her patient and munificent teacher, but he was a Skywatcher, and too much of his time was devoted to divination.

Elder Vasya stood rigidly, his mouth a down-turned line, as Zeneba mounted the step, turned, and sat in the hard seat.

All eyes were upon her, wide with surprise at the sudden presence of their long-grieving *mara*. She gazed back at them with a hard face.

"What news?"

The warriors and councilors looked about themselves for a moment, unsure what to say to her. Their hesitation aggravated her. It wasn't as if she were a *buna* rock that would turn to dust if not handled gently. Though, even as she thought this, she shivered. She clasped her hands into one big fist on her lap, musing what a lonely place her seat was.

One of the warriors, named Samuka, took a step forwards and bowed.

"Bless your name, Golden One. We are heartened to see you."

Swallowing hard, she bid him tell her his news.

"I came directly to tell you that our sabotage attempts have worked effectively. The demons cannot use the mines, and our tampering should keep them from mining at least until springtime."

"That *is* good news," Elder Vasya said.

Samuka looked at him quickly. He continued addressing Zeneba.

"With your permission, Golden One, I should like to continue. This seems to be keeping the demons from pushing further south."

"Indeed. Whatever means necessary, captain, if it keeps the demons from using our own resources against us," said Elder Vasya.

Samuka once more looked awkwardly between the Elder and Zeneba and chose to nod at the empty space between them.

Zeneba ground her teeth, the mere sound of the Elder's voice kindling in her a heat she had scarcely dared to feel in a long while. Her gaze slid over to him so that she might give him a sidelong glare.

"You have your wish, captain," she said. "Do what you can in the north, but see that you are home before the frosts come."

Elder Vasya's mouth was open, as if to protest, but Samuka said quickly, "It will be done, Golden One."

"May Nahara and Undin smile upon you."

Samuka bowed low again but did not depart.

"Is there something else, Brave One?"

"Yes. I . . . " He looked about quickly as if trying to find the words. "I must tell you, Golden One, that while we have been successful, it has been at a price."

"What do you mean?"

"On our last raid, we . . . Yaro was captured. He was struck in the side by one of the demon's weapons, and we could not get to him. They took him back to their city. We do not know what has happened to him."

Zeneba's bottom lip had begun to quiver during

this speech. Tears from the dregs of her soul sprung into her eyes.

She wouldn't have let Yaro go north either, knowing that if something happened, she wouldn't be able to bear it. She hadn't been able to keep him in Karak, despite her wishes. Though he was silent about it, Zaynab's death had cut Yaro to his core, and the only salve he had to put on the wound was watching Zeneba withdraw into the safety of her grief, leaving a sullen, hard exterior. This he could not bear.

As the reality of his fate sunk in, she felt her hands begin to tremble and her heart drummed painfully in her chest. She almost couldn't hear Samuka as he implored, "Forgive us, Golden One. We are ashamed to have left him. We wish to see if we can rescue him. We will not rest until he has been recovered."

Samuka's kneeling form was blurry through her tears. They began rolling down in large beads, splashing onto her clasped hands.

The sudden stab of pain in her abdomen made her double over, and she threw her hands over her face, her forehead pressing against her knees. Yaro had been a constant in her life since she had come to Karak, and she could fain recollect a time he hadn't been by her side.

She could feel Ondra beside her, her sudden outburst scaring him most of all. He would have touched her, comforted her, but she waved off his hand.

"Damn them," she murmured.

"Are you—?"

She shook her head.

Yaro's face the night Zaynab died flashed into her mind, contorted in anguish. If for no other reason they had been united in their grief, for Zaynab had been dear to them both. She had selfishly believed for a long while that she was the only one who suffered, but Yaro did too, though he bore it in silence.

Never had he let on how he hurt, or how she

prolonged his pain. She saw it now, in his face right before he left for the north. She had been blind. All she could think of was Yaro chained in a cold cell, the dark stretching long fingers to claim him, and she powerless to help him.

"It seems foolhardy, attempting to take on the demons for one rescue," Elder Vasya was saying. "Noble as it is, and much as we all want to see Yaro returned, it jeopardizes the success of our campaign."

Zeneba's head shot up indignantly at this. "He would walk into an abyss to rescue you," she snapped.

"You perhaps, Golden One, but certainly not me."

"I would for him," she said, her voice cracking. Tremors threatened to wrack her body again.

"No one here is disputing your loyalty to him. Yet it is not you being asked to rescue him."

His color changing to deep red, Samuka said, "We will gladly rescue him for the *mara*. Who else do we represent if not her?"

Touched by her warriors' commitment, Zeneba dried her eyes and sat straight, hoping to appear at least a little dignified.

"You bless me, Brave Ones," she said, bowing her head to them.

Samuka's eyes widened at the honor, and he and his warriors were quick to their knees.

"We are all touched by—indeed, Yaro would be pleased with your loyalty, but there is the fact that you cannot do this, Golden One."

Her face darkened. "What do you mean?"

"You are not, technically, *mara*. I am the head councilor, and for the time being, it is my order they must follow. I cannot risk this. Yaro is lost to us, and you must accept it."

"You would leave him to—"

"I would sacrifice him, yes! For the safety of all of us. And he would want it that way."

Zeneba felt something bubbling in the pit of her stomach, a white hotness that surged to her head. It was an unnerving sensation, one that heated and cooled her all at once. She couldn't hear such things. Yaro wasn't lost. He could be saved. He had to be.

And there was only one thing to do.

"Very well. If it must be a *mara*'s word they heed, then I am *mara*. I take back my seat. I am the daughter of Nahara and Undin, and I will be the one to lead my people."

Elder Vasya matched her hostile look, turning only his head towards her to say, "By all means, *lead them then*."

Her lip twitched.

The rest of the Hall had gone still, watching the drama between the two. The empty space between them seemed to spark. Zeneba's swirls of iridescent skin, the pattern different for every Charneki, which had for the past cycle remained ashen with sorrow, rippled into a hot red.

"You would risk our success over one—?" Elder Vasya stopped at her uninhibited flash of crimson rage.

"See what can be done, captain," she ordered. "Bring him back."

Samuka and the warriors, shining in their customary maroon, the color of bravery, said in unison, "It will be done!"

Samuka and his outfit eagerly headed from the Red Hall to prepare for their return journey. Elder Vasya was quick to follow, talking to no one and no one daring to speak to him.

Zeneba and Ondra were left alone in the Hall before long.

"Let me go with them," he implored.

She looked up at him, suddenly pained. "I didn't think you cared for Yaro."

He seemed hurt, and though she was sorry for insulting him, she knew exactly why she had.

"Then you know me very little."

He turned to walk from the Hall as well, his hue turning a saddened blue. When seeing his back, she was overcome with terror at being left alone.

"Ondra!" she cried. "Please, Ondra, don't leave me."

He returned quickly, kneeling before her. Clutching her wrists, he looked up into her face. "I'd go nowhere without your blessing."

She looked down at her lap and grasped his hands in hers. "I can't lose you too."

2

"I'm gonna go on a walk—just be a few minutes. You'll be all right?"

Rhys O'Callahan waved off Yue Tanaka, the store manager, knowing that he could handle the perhaps two people that would come into the store during her absence.

When she left, he was left alone in the store. It wasn't very big, about two-thousand square feet, and most of its shelves were empty by now. All people would have to pick from was what flavor of protein pack they wanted.

There were about half a dozen similar stores, distributed equally around the market quadrant.

His and another were the closest to the residential quadrant, while the others were similarly close to the other two quadrants. During the warmer months, they had had quite a bit to sell, such as bread, bags of rice, a few native fruits and greens, and some other necessities. Now most of the foodstuffs were out of season and they hadn't gotten a shipment from the farming colony in a while.

He had requested this reassignment. It got boring most of the time, but Rhys was good at keeping himself occupied, and Yue rarely noticed or reprimanded him for making pyramids out of the bags of rice. She was very hands-off, making her infinitely better than Hugh.

His mood soured at the thought of his brother. Sometimes he let himself think that it wasn't all Hugh's fault, that he hadn't known, was trying to protect him, but Rhys's bitterness was stronger than this inclination.

Zaynab had been his friend. They had never turned to violence, not even at their first meeting, and they had been proof that the regime's policy of violent opposition to the natives was unnecessary. Understanding was possible. At least, it had been.

With the natives thoroughly driven back, the regime had had little to occupy itself with other than policing its own people. Curfews were strict and there was little privacy. The military knew what everyone did and when they did it. Even he was finding it hard to take his walks past the perimeter.

Seemingly contrary to this, they did allow for occasional public forums, though Rhys didn't have to look hard to see this was just a safety valve. The regime relied on the legendary slowness of the democratic process—not that the forums were ever productive enough to even get that far.

It was all very frustrating, and he had given up on the idea of anything changing quickly. The regime would have its way—for now at least.

Looking about the empty store, Rhys pulled out his reader, a device which projected a foot-long screen. It had access to the Central Intelligence Unit, which contained all of Earth-knowledge. He bypassed this and went for the photo bank.

He scrolled through these often. It was filled with pictures of his weeks learning from Zaynab. There was them exploring the flatlands to the south. There was them riding his turtle-like creature, called a *garan*. There was them smiling up into the camera, days before he died.

Perhaps some of the most interesting pictures were those Zaynab had taken. Rhys had given him Hugh's unused reader, the Charneki loving the idea of picture-taking. He had taken it back with him to the native encampment and, when he could, turned the reader's lens on his surroundings.

He captured warriors training, sharpening weapons, riding *garans*. Rhys's favorites, though, were when Zaynab stole images of those closest to him. Rhys recognized several pictures of the big warrior—he had been the one who attacked Rhys, thinking he meant Zaynab harm, the night of the raid. Other pictures were of a tall, graceful Charneki, usually seated and staring off into the distance, as if there were a lot on her mind. He couldn't help but guess it was Zaynab's sister, Zeneba.

He had come across Zaynab's reader when walking through the remnants of the Charneki camp. It must have dropped from his body during the chaos. Transferring the photos, he had destroyed the other reader and left it in the bottom of a deep, dry creek bed.

He didn't cry anymore when seeing the pictures. Now they just filled him with a sort of aching, yet he treasured them. As he swiped through them, he absentmindedly touched the jade circlet Zaynab gave him. He had said Rhys was Charneki now.

His head snapped up at the sound of the front door opening, and his reflexes were quick, replacing the reader into his pocket.

Cassandra Tran, Hugh's friend, came striding towards him, wearing a pleasant smile. Of what he knew about Hugh's life during the seven-year journey, Cass was the only part Rhys liked. She didn't threaten to use him for target practice.

"What's up?" she said, leaning her arms on the counter.

"Nothing much."

"What've you been up to? Anything fun?"

"Not really."

"Such a vocabulary," she teased.

He would have taken offense had it been anyone else. Cass's grin, he was sure, could disarm anyone.

"So are you liking this job?"

"It's all right," he said with a shrug. "It's pretty easy and Yue's nice."

She was nodding along to his words, but he couldn't help feeling she had something to tell him.

"Did you need something today? We've only really got protein packs right now."

She shook her head and leaned in closer. "Do you think you'd have time for an extra job?"

"Extra job?" he repeated.

"Mm hmm." She looked about before continuing quietly, "Dr. Oswald is putting together a project, and he wants you to help him."

"Me? What for?"

The sound of doors opening made Cass shut her mouth quickly, and they both peered around to see Yue reentering the store.

She looked at them, surprised.

"Hi there," said Cass with that disarming smile.

Looking about quickly, she grabbed up the nearest handful of protein packs and put them in front of Rhys.

Mechanically he counted them and made a note in Cass's ration-book, a program embedded into all the readers. That was the way people got items, their "shopping" tracked by the book. All of them were allotted a certain amount of any given thing. No one was sure how long this would last, for there was no move to switch to some sort of money-based economy yet.

Once Yue moved into the back to open up the last boxes of inventory, Cass leaned in close again. "Come to our department office once you're off. He'll be expecting you, okay?"

Rhys couldn't find anything to say before Cass was bouncing back out of the store.

He hadn't made any sense of it even after he had helped Yue open up the last of the boxes, not after putting all the remaining inventory on the shelves, not even as he watched the minutes tick by until closing time.

Taking his coat off the hangar and bidding good-bye to Yue, Rhys left the store and headed along a somewhat unfamiliar route to the industrial quadrant, where the science department was. He needed no directions getting there, but was stalled by a guard at the entrance.

Once he was cleared and on his way again, he asked directions from a competent looking woman. She sent him directly to a small building full of what looked like offices, next to a much bigger structure that stood four stories tall. He entered the smaller one and from there was directed to Dr. Oswald's office.

He was all the way down, the side nearest the neighboring building. The hallway was chrome metal, having been made from some section or another of one of the starships.

Walking to the threshold, Rhys could hear Dr. Oswald talking quietly on the other side. As he put his hand up to knock, he heard the doctor saying, "Yes, it should go just like you want. I think it's safe to bet they'll take the bait—they'd be stupid not to."

His knock made the doctor stop short, and he looked up, the screen reflected in his glasses. Rhys thought he saw a projected face, but it was gone before he could really think about it.

"Ah, Rhys, good—sorry about that, I was just finalizing some things."

The doctor smiled quickly and stood, asking Rhys to come in and take a seat. Dr. Oswald's office wasn't large, though, when Rhys thought about it, there wasn't really any reason for it to be. He did all his important work in the lab, which Rhys assumed was the neighboring building.

"I'm glad you came," the doctor started. "I have something that might interest you."

"Cass mentioned an extra job?"

"Yes, that's one way to look at it. Honestly you might be able to give up the store altogether if you'd like—that is, if you take my offer."

"And what's that?"

Dr. Oswald smirked at Rhys's sauciness.

"I'd like you to come on as my apprentice."

Rhys balked. "Why?"

Leaning back in his chair, Dr. Oswald regarded him for a moment.

"You're a remarkable boy, Rhys, befriending a native when anyone else would have just killed them on the spot."

Rhys went cold. "How . . . ?"

"Readers are easy things to hack, and General

Hammond has a tendency to pry—she likes to know what's going on, you see. But I insisted that rather than punishing you, you could be put to better use."

The doctor's calmness was having the opposite effect on Rhys. He had to stop himself from twitching or chewing on his lower lip.

"What I'm suggesting, Rhys, is that you help me—help *us* better understand the native species."

"I thought you were only interested in killing them."

"Fair enough. Yes, taking the offensive is working for the time being. However, even General Hammond can't expect that to last forever. We're hoping to switch to a more . . . diplomatic approach. No one wants to mark the beginning of our new lives here with genocide."

"And how're you going to do that?"

"We must learn about the natives—their customs, their beliefs, their language. It will help us come up with a long-term plan for the future. I believe there are other solutions than violence, Rhys. The natives are wonderful creatures—we should be studying them, not killing them."

Rhys nodded, marveling that someone else could feel the same way as he did.

"They're really amazing," Rhys said.

"I want you to tell me all about them, Rhys, and if you come aboard, I hope we can learn more together. We have to understand our new home, and that includes the natives."

"I don't really know what I could do for you," Rhys admitted. "I'm not good at science."

"I'm not asking you to be."

Pulling a small device out of his pocket, Dr. Oswald pressed a few buttons and a large projection filled some of the empty space between them. On it Rhys saw himself—at eleven—with some statistics and notes next to the picture.

"You were tested before boarding the *Mayflower* for skill sets and traits."

He pressed another button and there were two identical projections.

"Your brother tested into an engineering apprenticeship, scoring high in problem solving, math, and reasoning."

Rhys ground his teeth at having to remember.

"Your own skill set was very different," the doctor said, "but that doesn't mean it was necessarily worse. You also scored high in problem solving, were fluent in three languages, and exhibited, for lack of a better term, tenacity. While not necessarily useful aboard ship, these are all perfect qualities for what I'm proposing."

Rhys's chest swelled from all the praise, though he didn't know what to do with it.

"Work with me, and put these skills to good use," said Dr. Oswald, reaching a hand over the desk.

Rhys looked at the hand then the person it was attached to. He didn't know quite what to think.

Glancing at the two stats sheets, he began

to relish the thought of doing something Hugh couldn't. He took Dr. Oswald's hand.

"When should we start?"

––––––––––

Morning shift was Elena Ames's least favorite shift. Not exactly a morning person, she continued rubbing her eyes as she made her way into the prison compound.

Well, 'compound' might have been an exaggeration, but that's what the general called it. In reality it was little more than a normal sized building that housed a monitoring station in the front, a small kitchen, and two dozen cells. The irony wasn't lost on Elena that the cells had been repurposed from rooms of one of the starships' Apprentice Blocks.

Upon entering, she headed for a small set of lockers on the left side of the room. In the second one, she traded her jacket for a gun and holster.

She exchanged cool nods with Markus Ruskakov,

the soldier sitting at the monitoring station. Markus had been a fellow military apprentice during the journey. He had gotten quite large, which he always used to his advantage if he could.

Putting her hand on the scanner, the door to the inner room of the prison slid open. All it consisted of was a long hall with a dozen Plexiglas doors on each side with block letters painted on them.

It felt a bit odd to be on guard duty, though she had been assigned to it for several months now. They hadn't even had a prison compound during their first months on Terra Nova, but as General Hammond's influence had grown, she saw fit to build one, using materials that otherwise would have gone to housing. It sat empty and unused for a long while, but now that it housed a few prisoners, it was necessary to assign a squad to guard duty.

In the cell to her immediate left she found a familiar face.

"You here again?"

Ulysses Carter looked up at her and grinned. "Can't help myself," he said.

Carter had become a regular in the compound, held usually no more than three days. As there were no official laws, he couldn't be held for breaking any, but still it seemed to give General Hammond some satisfaction to throw him in jail, even if only for a day.

"What're you in for now?"

"The usual—'causing social unrest,' as she likes to put it."

"Led another rally, did you?"

"All I'm doing is drumming up support. We're already a majority, but the more support we have, the better." He peered up at her. "Everyone's welcome to come, you know."

Elena cleared her throat. "I'll keep that in mind."

She was saved from having to defend her vague answer by a loud voice at the end of the hall. Elena turned to see Oscar Livermore pounding a fist against the last door on the right.

"You hear me in there? Huh? I asked if you heard me, you motherf—"

"Hey!" Elena called, jogging down the hall.

He saw her hand on her holster and glared.

"Get outta here," she growled. "You're done."

Turning his hateful eyes back on the prisoner inside the last cell, he growled, "Don't know why we're keeping this alive. No point."

He slammed his fist against the glass again before finally stalking down the hall and out the door. Elena watched him go the whole way, only turning her gaze away when the door had slid closed.

When she looked at the prisoner, she beheld a very sad sight. The native was ill-suited for the cell. He was about eight-and-a-half feet tall, so whenever he stood, his head almost touched the ceiling. The slab that served as the bed was far too small and took up much of the floor space so that he was crammed between it and the opposite wall when he wanted to lie down.

He was sitting on the slab, his folded body

making various sharp angles. His elbows rested on his knees, his intertwined hands balled up in front of his face. He looked impossibly tired, his square eyes puffed and bleary, and his color grayer than perhaps normal.

It always took Elena's breath away to see him up close. For so long humans had thought they were alone in the universe. No such luck. Though there were stark differences between them, it amazed her that there were also similarities. Vast distances and yet life still looked remarkably the same.

He gazed at her steadily, measuring her. His irises were almost bluish.

"Sorry about that," she said.

He of course didn't understand her, but seemed interested in her softer tone.

"Oscar can be a real ass," she found herself saying, "but you shouldn't mind him. He's a lot of bark, and honestly a lot of bite, but I think you could take him."

That certainly wasn't a lie. While the natives

were thin, almost spindly—his shoulders were narrower than Elena's—they still had lean, rippling muscle underneath their thick gray hide.

They knew he was a warrior. He had been captured during a native raid on the mines, and Elena had first seen him wearing a russet colored breastplate and other pieces of armor. His weapons—a sword, metal spear, shield, and assorted daggers—had already been handed over to the science department. He looked the warrior too; scars, big and small, adorned his body, from a few on his legs and arms, to several on his chest, and even a crescent shaped one next to his left eye.

"Sorry about the . . . " She indicated the purpling bruises on his shoulders and chest. He even had a cut lip. Those were new.

He muttered something short, and her interest piqued at hearing the native language. She had heard snippets before, but those were all shouted orders. It was fascinating now to listen to the words in a quieter, more normal voice.

She got little else from him in the ensuing hours, though she rarely left his cell during her shift. It was just her in the long hall, one soldier seeming sufficient to guard two prisoners, yet she couldn't help but dislike leaving the native on his own, not after Oscar.

When her stomach growled, she took a protein pack out of her back pocket and began chewing. She had grown so used to the bars by now that she didn't taste it—not that there was much to taste.

She glanced down and saw that most of the food he had been given was untouched and wondered if it was out of protest or that he truly couldn't eat it. The second idea worried her, thinking he might begin to wither away.

She held up her protein pack. "I'd offer you some, but honestly it's pretty damn terrible. I'm sparing you really."

He looked at the bar then to her and grunted. She didn't blame him for not thinking it food.

While continuing to chew, she told him, "It's

kinda crazy, really—we didn't think you'd even exist. Thought we'd have the planet to ourselves. That's how it was—on our planet, that is. We don't know how to handle competition."

She couldn't really say why she was jabbering on—jabbering certainly wasn't something she liked to do, but it felt good in a way. Soldiering was a lot of keeping silent and taking orders, and since she rarely saw her friends, it was good to say something, if only to make sure her voice still worked. Not only this, but she hoped the native might be a little more at ease if at least one of his guards was cordial, not pounding on his door.

"I'd like to know your name," she said after her last bit of protein pack, "but even if you said it, I probably wouldn't know . . . so can I call you Steve?"

She peered at him, expecting some sort of answer, but got little more than a stare.

"I'm just gonna call you Steve. Do you have any family, Steve? A wife and kids?"

The native continued to look on with a sort of bemused apathy.

"Yeah, you seem more like a lifetime bachelor to me. The rugged type."

She spent the rest of her shift trying to guess his life, creating a rather elaborate backstory which saw him in a rags-to-riches scenario. Humble but brave of heart, he had probably risen quickly through the ranks and was now the most esteemed warrior in his squad.

"Sound about right?" she asked.

He had his head leaned back against the wall. His eyes were closed.

"All right then," she said, taking the hint.

Her replacement came soon after, though he stayed towards the other end of the hall. She didn't say anything more to the native, though his eyes had cracked open and he was peering at her. She gave him a nod and headed out.

On her way her gauntlet began to flash blue. Looking down, she saw an updated order.

"Looks like you're sprung," she told Carter when she got to his cell.

Entering the combination on the order into the control panel beside the cell door, the Plexiglas slid open.

Carter stood up and stretched.

Elena wished he would look a little less self-satisfied, at least until they were out. He was making the new guard glower. She walked out with Carter, stalling for a moment when she got her jacket and left her gun.

"That native in there," Carter said.

She looked up at him, surprised. His eyes were narrowed slightly with a thought, and she realized he had been waiting to speak on it.

"He's interesting."

"Get home," Elena said, "and keep out of trouble."

Carter laughed, a deep, rumbling sound.

"Sure, little miss. Anything you say."

Sitting down at one of the outdoor tables lining the city square, Hugh rubbed his eyes and wondered if it would be possible to get his hands on a caffeine shot. He mourned the idea that the colony wouldn't be growing coffee beans or tea leaves or really anything any time soon. Being up in the daytime was a little surreal to him. Everything was so bright.

The Terra Novan day was long. The planet was on a 27-hour orbit, and now that it was late autumn, the nights were finally lengthening. This was actually good news for Hugh—he might catch a few hours of darkened sleep.

He had agreed to get up early—fourteen-hundred hours instead of sixteen-hundred hours—so that he could meet Elena and Cass for dinner; well, dinner for them, breakfast for him. At twenty-one-hundred hours, he would head down with Saranov and the others to see what more could be done for the mining equipment. It was beginning to look like they would have to scrap most of it and begin again.

"Well, don't you look like the epitome of liveliness."

He propped his head on his hand and grinned up at Cass.

"It's so early," he said.

She laughed at this and sat down.

"So how's work going?"

"Pretty great, actually," she said. "We're starting a new project."

She didn't offer up what the project was, and Hugh knew better than to ask. She could rarely talk about what the science department was doing nowadays. In truth, Hugh wasn't supposed to discuss his work either. Sabotage at the mines was 'bad press,' as General Hammond called it.

"It'll keep you pretty busy?"

"Hopefully. I'm really excited about it—it'll do a lot of good, I think," she said with a smile.

He wasn't offended by her secrecy; it was part of their jobs, and he knew from her smile that she really would like to tell him all about it. Aboard ship, he, Cass, and Elena had been thick as thieves.

Elena arrived as they were chatting about the horror of reverting back to protein packs. Hugh had to hide, as he always did, how truly happy he was to see her.

"Chalk is good for the digestive system," Cass was saying, "at least that's what I tell myself."

"What now?" Elena said, plopping down beside her.

"We're debating if there's a silver lining to protein packs."

"Ah. That's a definite no."

Hugh smirked. "At least they come in flavors."

"While I haven't eaten a lot of strawberries in my time, I think it's safe to say strawberry-flavored is a bit of a stretch," Cass said.

They would have continued berating the staple of their diet longer if they hadn't noticed the growing number of people in the square. While it wasn't abnormal for people to congregate on a clear autumn evening, no one was sitting down at tables or strolling. There was an excited buzz about the crowd, which was growing larger by the minute.

"I didn't know it was tonight," Cass remarked.

"What's tonight?" Hugh asked.

"The forum."

He had heard about the public meetings but had yet to see one. The main thing he knew about them was that little, if anything, ever got done. Elena had told him it was a lot of speech-making rather than action-taking.

"Should we stay?"

Cass shrugged at his question. "Might as well."

They continued gnawing on their protein pack dinners as the crowd began convening around one of the tables across the square.

The meeting was soon underway. A tall woman with short brown hair mounted the table and gazed out at the crowd.

"Thank you for coming," she projected. "It's

nice to see you all here. We've all come for the same reason—we want our voices heard!"

The crowd raised a cry of agreement.

"Hammond isn't doing what she promised. She was sworn, after getting here, to give democracy a try. Over a year and she still refuses to give over power. We're not on Earth anymore. We left all that behind us."

"This's supposed to be a new start!" someone called.

"Right! And instead we're in the same turmoil we were trying to get away from. We've had enough of dictators."

There were loud assertions and fists thrust into the air.

Hugh sat captivated. He had seen this crowd before—a year ago they had protested outside General Hammond's headquarters all night and received a rough reception in the morning. From the sound of it, their message hadn't changed, and neither had General Hammond's attitude towards them.

Their talk was fiery, and they made no effort to hide their disdain for both General Hammond and her army dogs. Hugh glanced over to see how Elena was taking such talk, and to his surprise, found her sitting quietly, listening.

"She's not just going to hand over power!" called someone, making their way to the front.

Hugh recognized the face but couldn't match it with a name.

"*Dammit*," he heard Elena mutter under her breath.

The newcomer joined the woman standing on the table. There were happy sounds at his arrival.

"Thought you'd been locked up, Carter. Again!" said the woman.

They all had a laugh at this.

"Just got sprung, actually," Carter said. "What've I missed?"

The woman opened her mouth to reply, but was cut off by someone saying, "Nothing that hasn't already been said."

"I'd say you're not feeling the cause tonight, Paul," said Carter.

"I feel it all right—I'm just tired of hearing the same speech. You get us inspired, talk big talk, and then get yourself thrown in prison. Are we supposed to follow you there?"

"Certainly not. There're only twenty-two other unused cells."

There was a small rumble of laughter from the crowd, but the atmosphere had simmered. Carter saw this and tried to get them back on track.

"Paul has a point," he said. "It's past the time for talk. We've got to take action. She's not going to give up power—we're going to have to take it from her."

"So you keep saying," another piped up. "But how?"

"We outnumber her military personnel ten to one."

"Are you suggesting we hit Headquarters? All-out coup? Should we guillotine her while we're at it?"

"She calls us civilians, so we handle this like civilians. We start making our own laws, policing ourselves, forming our own government. She has as much power as we give her."

"I'd call her guns power."

"Even I don't think the general would fire on us—a queen must have subjects," said Carter. "Without us, she has no excuse for her poorly disguised war on the natives, and without that, she doesn't have any legs to stand on."

3

Zeneba sat in her seat with her legs crossed and her shoulders stiff. She knew it was inappropriate, yet she remained haughty as the delegates entered the Red Hall.

She couldn't help her obvious disdain. Not in three hundred cycles had the Tikshi been allowed into the Red City, peacefully or no. Her predecessor, Harva the Golden-Faced, had had five successful campaigns against these barbarians, keeping them out of Charneki land. Indeed, all Charneki rulers, dating back to Yalah the Gold-Fisted, had kept the Tikshi banished to the southern islands.

All Charneki had been told of Yalah's glorious

campaign as *mahiim*. In a time of great crisis, when the Tikshi were overrunning Charnek, Yalah had united the clans and drove them further and further south until they were forced to cross the treacherous straits, known as Umarr's Finger. Seeing they were thoroughly defeated, the Tikshi pleaded mercy from Yalah, which he granted, though they were forbidden thereafter to cross Umarr's Finger into Charnek.

Always devious, the Tikshi did not long abide their promise and soon tried to reclaim territory along the southern coast. This was their constant goal, and every reign saw a new Tikshi campaign, followed swiftly by a new agreement that they would stay on their island—known to Charneki as Prrarnek, or Traitor's Land—and relinquish any ambitions toward Charnek.

Zeneba believed this long, treacherous history a good enough reason to receive the Tikshi delegates as she did. She was glad, at the moment, that Elder Zhora, her reinstated head councilor, was blind, for he surely would have reprimanded her. She felt a little justified, however, seeing how stiff and suspicious her council became upon the entrance of the delegates.

She had never actually seen a Tikshi before, only heard stories and seen mural depictions. She found them quite ugly. In some ways it was easy to see that the Tikshi were related to the Charneki, though it offended her to acknowledge this. They were lanky with long limbs and necks, yet they were stouter than Charneki, standing not as tall yet broader. Their skin lacked the beautiful swirls of iridescence. Whereas Charneki had nice, soft, elegant angles, the Tikshi were all hard, jaunty, with small dark eyes. Perhaps the greatest difference was where female Charneki had natural growths on their heads of skin and bone, called headdresses, the Tikshi had, at their jaw, on either side, protruding, thick tusks.

The delegates, eight in total, proceeded into the Red Hall, looking about as if expecting an attack.

No Charneki moved a muscle, indignant at the idea of blood staining the Red Hall.

Zeneba swallowed hard, anxious as they moved closer. She knew she was in no danger; Ondra and others of the Guard stood close by, yet there was something dangerous about these Tikshi. She didn't like their looks.

The delegates halted a few steps from the dais. A prolonged pause engulfed the Red Hall as the Charneki waited for the delegates to bow to their *mara*.

Finally the lead Tikshi bowed his head slightly, as if it refused to go lower, and said in a coarse accent, "Greetings, noble lady. We're pleased you are seeing us."

"You will address the *mara* with appropriate deference, Master Par-lum," growled Elder Jeska. "She is not a mere 'lady,' she is *mara*, the Golden One, child of Nahara and Undin."

The Tikshi, Par-lum, looked Zeneba up and down.

"She doesn't look golden to me," he said.

Some Elders gasped at the offense while others shook their heads and scowled. Ondra took a step forward, itching for retribution. Zeneba herself only frowned, knowing Par-lum was baiting her.

The Tikshi finally released her gaze to assess the rest of the council. He seemed amused by the general outrage.

"Forgive me, *mara*; I don't know all of your . . . fine ways. In Prrarnek 'lady' is a fine title."

"You're not in Prrarnek," Ondra hissed.

Zeneba raised a hand to bring silence to the Hall.

"You, of course, cannot be expected to know all our ways, Master Par-lum," she said. "You are forgiven, and must be commended for knowing our language as well as you do, though I must say, your accent could use some refinement."

Par-lum was between a smile and a sneer as he said, "You know best, *mara*."

"Shall we start, then, with why you have come?"

He took half a step forward. "News has reached us in the south of these stars with demons inside. We come to know if this is true."

She hesitated. "Yes, it is."

"Has anything been done?"

"We are keeping them in the north for now," she said, "but this is none of your concern."

"I disagree," said Par-lum. "The Tikshi think this very much our business. You fine Charneki try to forget, but we Tikshi are part of this world too. For this reason we want an alliance. Together we destroy these demons."

"You know nothing of them, Master Par-lum. These demons are like nothing anyone, Charneki or Tikshi, has ever seen. Their weapons are mysterious and destructive and make ours seem useless."

One of Par-lum's eyes narrowed, making Zeneba feel as though she had misspoken. Elder Zhora put a hand on the armrest of the seat.

"It's a wonder, then, that you have stood against them."

"They have their weaknesses," she said.

"It seems good, then, that we've come. Together we can overwhelm them with numbers, even with their better weapons. If you agree to alliance, we would stand with you."

While the idea was a good one, something about Tikshi warriors lining up alongside Charneki didn't put Zeneba at ease.

"At what price?" asked Elder Vasya, coming forward. His hands were behind him, and his look was suspicious. "You cannot expect us to believe the arrival of the demons has suddenly made you sympathetic."

"I don't know this word, 'sympathetic,'" said Par-lum, "but I swear our Chieftain Treya wants alliance."

"Oh, I am sure he does," said Elder Vasya. "What are his terms? There is always something."

Par-lum's gaze slid over to Elder Vasya as his lips curled up. "I'll forgive you and not be insulted. You can think what you like, but that won't help you against the demons. Alliance could be your only answer."

Elder Zhora leaned in close to Zeneba and whispered, "Hear him."

"I am grateful for your Chieftain's concern. Indeed, you are right to remind us that you are part of this world, and you are right to want to defend it," Zeneba said, her face softening a little. "I am willing to discuss your alliance"—though the idea revolted her—"if there are no terms."

Par-lum wore a small smirk. "I didn't say that, *mara*."

Zeneba's heart skipped a beat and her mouth slackened. To disregard her good will so quickly!

Taking a step forward, the Tikshi said, "We are, as you say, willing to defend our land. But we have little land. We want room to breathe," he said over Elder Vasya's indignant scoffs, "for our island grows very small. Let us cross Umarr's Finger, and we'll stand with you."

Elder Vasya let out a scornful laugh. "I expected no less from a Tikshi!"

"For once I agree with the Elder," said Zeneba, her face all hard lines again. "We have lost enough of our home to the demons—I will not see more taken by you. If you have other terms we can discuss, then please, say so; otherwise, I fear we have exhausted the topic."

Par-lum ground his teeth. "That land was our home before you damned Charneki stole it from us!"

"Watch your tongue, Prarri!" Ondra bellowed.

Par-lum's gaze flicked to Ondra and he almost laughed. "Will you, honorable and hospitable *mara*, set your *porra* on me now?"

"You will not be touched," Zeneba hissed, "for *we* are people of our word."

"So you would rather share land with demons?" he demanded. "Will you make alliance with *them*?"

She clenched her jaw, not letting her skin ripple into fiery red with sheer will. "I will never deal

71

with them—they are murderers. But you, you are not much better. You come to me, asking to break your oath. You have no honor."

Par-lum's nostrils flared dangerously. "You are thieves and usurpers—anything else you claim to be is lies! You can't speak of honor!"

Elder Zhora was grasping at her arm, imploring, "Please, Golden One, please, this is rash. You must think—what they offer is great and ask for in return little."

"*Little!*" Zeneba stood indignantly, out of the Elder's reach. "My ancestors cannot have been mistaken—every *mar* and *mara* has heard this agreement of theirs, and every one has turned them away. I will not bow when they stood."

Elder Zhora sank down in his seat and remained silent. His stooped shoulders were almost enough to quell the fire burning in Zeneba. But she was determined. Already she was marked—she was the first *mara* to deal with such a new threat. She already seemed weak in the eyes of her council. She had paid for her mistakes with her brother's life. She wouldn't risk the Charneki in the south or the pride of her ancestors for a promised alliance with these barbarians.

Par-lum glowered, though he seemed to be collecting his wits. The other Tikshi had grouped together protectively, but as the Hall fell into a deafening silence, their stances relaxed a little.

"I will not agree to your terms," said Zeneba. "You were foolish to think we would agree. If you have nothing else to discuss, I ask you to leave, for only allies of my seat are welcome in the Red Hall."

"You speak big words for a little girl, *mara*. Our chieftain won't suffer a little girl."

Ondra took a hasty step towards Par-lum. "Threaten the *mara* again and I'll have your head, Prrari."

Par-lum gave him another smiling sneer. "Do that, boy, and your little *mara* will have two wars, if she doesn't already."

"Ondra," she said, her voice purposefully measured, "stand down."

He returned a few paces from her side and remained quiet, though he didn't seem sorry.

"Again I say that if you have nothing else to speak on, I shall have you returned to your boats. Tell your chieftain of my decision and see if he might find something else we can discuss. Until then, leave the demons to us."

Par-lum twisted his head and neck to the side rather than bowing it before he turned and left the Red Hall, the others following. He left in his wake a dead silence, even after he had disappeared from sight.

Elder Zhora didn't wait long. "He was right, Zeneba—the alliance could be the only answer. You should not have sent him away."

"I'm not in the mood to be scolded, Skywatcher," she said quietly, her formal accent slipping into her old rural lilt.

The fire had left her. She was tired and wanted desperately to adjourn the meeting.

"I do not mean to scold, only advise. You are *mara* and your judgment is to be trusted. I speak to you only as a friend."

"I know that, but I wouldn't insult you to call the likes of them my friends too."

The Skywatcher took a heavy breath. "Nahara showed me a plant," he said, and all within earshot hushed. "The plant was made up of two branches, sharing a stem. With one lightning strike, it was cleft in two. From one of the branches a hideous new plant grew."

Zeneba's head fell into her hands. "I wish you'd told me your vision before."

He shook his head. "Nahara only shows me what will come to be. I did not understand what it meant until now."

"What does she mean by this vision?"

"The stem has been cleft—there is no mending it," he said. "Now, I fear, something terrible will grow. You must be wary, Zeneba. No good will come of this. The Tikshi's ambition is growing past our control, and the demons present them with opportunity."

"Well it is not as if we have made a *new* enemy," Elder Vasya said.

"Perhaps not," the Skywatcher said, "but they will prove a new threat."

———

Rhys made no secret of how excited he was to get started on Dr. Oswald's project. He had quite literally jumped out of bed and raced from the apartment, stalling only long enough to throw a clean shirt and boots on. He was almost jittery when he entered the prison compound with the doctor.

They met one of the guards at the monitoring station who proceeded to spout regulations and procedure, all of which was white noise to Rhys's ear. Once the speech was over, a door in the back left corner of the room slid open, and they walked into the block.

The long hall stretched out a ways with a dozen rooms on each side. At the end stood, to his surprise, Elena.

She greeted them with a stiff nod.

"How's he doing today?" asked Dr. Oswald.

Elena took a quick look inside the cell. "Just fine. A little grumpy."

Rhys found that an odd thing to say, but he couldn't question her about it, for she, with another glance at the native, moved aside to give them room.

Dr. Oswald didn't seem to notice the remark, too excited to see the native up close again. He himself had overseen the native when he had first arrived and had assigned a doctor to see to the wounds he sustained.

He had all the information they knew about the natives on a classified file, which Rhys had been allowed to see for the sake of addition and correction. Scans and tests had been run on the native, and the file contained analysis of his blood, brain activity, and X-rays of his different internal systems. Dr. Oswald was absolutely fascinated by the native's blue blood and organs, some of which seemed similar to human ones, though Charneki had several others with uses that had yet to be determined.

Dr. Oswald stepped up first and took a good long look. He smiled.

"He's healing up nicely. I'd wager more quickly than we would."

He continued to gaze steadily inside the cell, said a few other things, waited. Finally he stepped back.

"We'll need him to talk if we want to add to the DL."

The DL, Dialect Library, was a handheld device used back on Earth to help translate languages. The device could pick up not only words but inflections, sounds, patterns. Using these the DL identified which language it was and, if it knew it already, translated it into a desired second language. If it was a language the device was unfamiliar with, it tracked the words and patterns of the language, putting it through various algorithms until it could be deciphered.

So far the DL only contained what Rhys knew of the Charneki language, which he admitted was very little. His additions were mostly single words rather than whole sentences, and even when he had been actively learning the language from Zaynab, he found syntax difficult.

"All right, Rhys, you're up."

Stepping forward, Rhys finally had the chance to look into the cell himself. To his surprise, he found a familiar face, though it was half turned from him. The native was Zaynab's big protector.

Not having interacted with a Charneki since Zaynab's death, he found himself breathless. The big warrior was magnificent. Solid, graceful, he was a sight to behold with his shimmering iridescent skin. He seemed unearthly in all senses of the word, and Rhys had to remind himself that it was the humans who were unearthly here.

The native's gaze slid over, and he peered at Rhys out of the corner of his eye, which widened at the sight of him. He turned his head a little. Rhys shivered as the recognition swept over him.

Rhys bowed his head to the native and said, "*Yan amar.*"

The native was surprised by the greeting, his hairless brows rising. He turned his body a bit more towards Rhys.

"*Boneer Charneki vanma-ni sua?*"

He could feel Dr. Oswald's excitement at the sound of the native's deep voice.

He didn't know some of the words, but from *Charneki vanma-ni,* or 'the Charneki language' he understood the question.

Rhys nodded and said, "*Loa,*" or 'small.'

The native continued to regard him curiously,

though he wore a scowl. He seemed interested in Rhys, yet still on his guard knowing there were other humans just out of sight. Rhys didn't blame him for being suspicious.

"*Kutnan nerma-buara Charneki vanma-ni sua?*"

Rhys had to think for a moment and referred to the DL for some words. It was able to translate *nerma*, 'how,' and he knew *sua* already as 'you,' and from this he was finally able to answer, "Zaynab."

The name had an immediate effect on the Charneki. His scowl melted, his eyes became distant. He hung his head.

Rhys sat down, hoping to catch the native's eye again. He leaned forward, his nose almost touching the Plexiglas.

"Where is Zaynab?" he asked, '*Humarr-bua Zaynab?*'

The native rubbed his eyes with a thumb and finger.

"*Ue dua.*"

He understood *ue* as the word for 'sleep.'

Rhys's stomach clenched, and he had the fleeting thought that he was going to be sick. He didn't want to understand what he meant. He knew, in his heart, what had happened to Zaynab, yet there was always part of him that hoped the wounds hadn't been fatal. He had hoped his sister would save him.

He lifted his head to find the native peering at him sidelong. They perfectly understood each other.

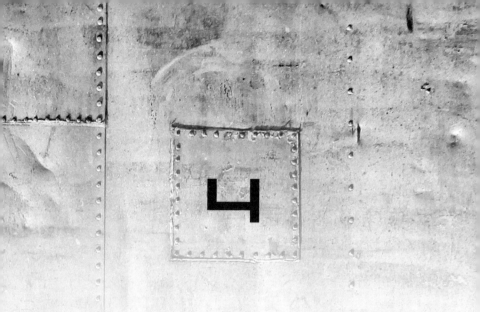

4

Hugh's back felt like it was made up of thousands of achy nerves all fraying at the ends. Rolling his shoulders didn't help, but he did it anyway.

He wished they could just be done with the mines. Nothing could be done. There had been another sabotage, but unlike the last one, no one had seen them come or go. He was starting to suspect they knew another way in. Winter was impending and the farming operation had been given up until the spring, everyone except a guard outfit brought back to New Haven.

He entered the apartment to find Rhys getting

ready for the day; running into him was actually becoming quite commonplace—though getting a word out of him was still rare.

Rhys seemed to barely notice Hugh coming in. He glanced at him sidelong before resuming his task. He was putting a reader, protein packs, and another device Hugh didn't recognize into a pack.

"Happy birthday," Hugh said.

The words hung in the air with a painful silence. Hugh almost winced. He had hoped, though he didn't know why, that the reminder of it being their birthday might get him something out of Rhys. In truth it wasn't technically their birthday. On Terra Nova it was November 12th, but since Terra Novan years were 159 days longer, it certainly wasn't on Earth. To accommodate the longer years, but to maintain some Earth-culture, there were still twelve months, but each was over forty days long.

Hugh watched Rhys for any sort of reaction.

His brother had paused but quickly recovered with a frown. He stayed silent.

"Thirteen's a big year," Hugh pressed on.

He knew he was wearing out his luck, if he had any to begin with at all, but he just couldn't help it. Rhys's silence ate at him until he felt raw. He knew their brotherhood was broken—he saw that every day. Yet each time he saw Rhys, he wanted to mend it, or at least try. During his seven years aboard ship, he had felt incomplete without his twin. Twin. That word felt foreign, hollow now. It made his heart feel bruised.

"I'm already thirteen," Rhys said.

"Well, yeah, but . . . " Hugh leaned against the sink. "Anyway. Did you want to, I don't know, do something today?"

"Why?"

Hugh opened his mouth and closed it. He didn't know why he let himself hope.

"I thought we could take the day off," Hugh

muttered, focusing on the ground, "and do something. Together."

"I have work."

"It's just a day. You can skip—they'll understand."

"No," Rhys said, giving him a hard look, "I can't."

"Why?"

"I just can't, okay? Drop it."

Rhys's tone, even with the age difference, shut Hugh up. He knew that voice well. It was imperious, demanding, threatening. It was the voice that had made Rhys king of the alleyways back on Earth. No kid messed with him, not if they were smart. That voice had gotten them out of scrapes and scared off would-be enemies. Hugh never liked when it turned on him.

Hugh shoved his hands in his pockets. Suddenly he felt agitated. He was older now and probably wiser. Yes, they were twins, at least they should be where it counted, but the reality was that Hugh was older. He shouldn't be talked to that way, and he told Rhys as much, though quietly.

Rhys glared at him from the corners of his eyes. Hugh knew that look too.

The look had the opposite effect on Hugh it usually did, and it shocked even him when he asked, "Why aren't you working at the store anymore?"

Rhys's glare slipped into surprise. "What?"

"You heard me."

Rhys turned towards him, putting his whole body behind a frown. He was starting to grow, just like Hugh had at his age, and was already getting quite broad around the shoulders. Hugh half suspected he would be taller than him.

But right now he wasn't, and Hugh utilized his taller frame to look authoritative. He even crossed his arms while he waited for an answer.

"What, are you checking up on me now?" Rhys demanded.

"This isn't about me," Hugh said. "What're

you getting up to? You say you can't miss work, but you're not going at all."

"I'm not working there anymore. But it's none of your business anyway."

"Where're you working then?"

Rhys's answer was to flip the cover over his pack and shoulder it. He gave Hugh a withering look as he made towards the door.

Hugh took a step forwards, which put him half in Rhys's way of the door and earned him another glare.

Changing tactics, he tried, more softly, "Look, Rhys, I'm not trying to check up on you or boss you around. I just want to know what's up. I wanted to make sure you're okay. You never talk to me, so I had to do it myself."

Rhys's glare dropped, but he didn't soften. Hugh thought he looked tired.

"I got a new job, okay?"

"What is it?"

"It's with the science department."

"Doing what?"

"Can't tell you."

That surprised him. "Why not?"

"I just can't. Will you leave it?"

In retrospect, Hugh should have stopped while he was ahead. But, heady with getting so many words out of Rhys, Hugh foolishly pressed on.

"Why can't you tell me? What's so important?"

Rhys looked at him venomously. "Don't act so innocent. You're job's not exactly an open book."

He couldn't argue with that, and Rhys, knowing he had the high ground, used Hugh's silence to escape.

The sound of the door closing brought Hugh back. Rather than feeling his normal, numb complacency, he was filled with hot agitation. How was it that Rhys always knew how to smack him around? It hadn't been so bad when they were kids, but he was twenty and being smart-mouthed by his little brother was getting old. No, it was downright insulting.

Fine then. If Rhys wasn't going to tell him, he would find out for himself. He was getting pretty good at it anyway.

———————

"It's not that I mind cold weather," Elena said, her head leaning against the wall, "it's just that your winters are freezing ass cold."

She looked over at Steve to see if he had anything to add. He was just giving her a look.

"You guys don't wear much clothing," she noted. "You must have pretty thick skin then, because let me tell you, it's freezing ass cold."

She chuckled at her own little joke since Steve wouldn't. There was still the obvious language barrier between them, though she had a growing interest in the translation project Cass, Rhys, and Dr. Oswald were working on. She tried not to let on, tried acting aloof whenever they were there, but she attentively listened.

Lately she had started looking forward to going to work. Guard duty could be mind-numbingly boring, but the prospect of talking with—well, more *at*, Steve perked her up. Sometimes she wondered if she was growing sympathetic to the natives. The idea made her uneasy, for it contradicted seven years of training: take orders unquestioningly, and her orders were to hate and distrust the natives.

She didn't hate Steve. He seemed like a nice . . . what word should she use? Being? Sure, he was a nice being. He didn't say much to her, but seemed to listen. Sometimes he nodded, sometimes he looked at her with what she liked to think was a bit of sass.

If she didn't hate Steve, did that mean she didn't hate the natives? She wasn't sure, and she didn't like to think about it. Her experience with them, with the exception of Steve, was shooting at them. That was following orders.

She stole a glance at Steve's wounds. He had sustained a gunshot wound to his side when he was captured—luckily it had been a glancing shot. He also had several, now fading, bruises that purpled his shoulders. The soldiers had been rough with him, and the regime would have hurt him more if the science department hadn't intervened.

The sight of the human-inflicted wounds made her feel guilty, like there was a rock weighing down her stomach. It recalled the first skirmish they had had with the natives. She had downed one, a shot straight to the chest. It hadn't suffered. She thought it hurt her more than it did the native.

That was soldiering, she tried to tell herself. But what would she do if the order came over her gauntlet to exterminate the native prisoner? The thought made her feel worse, and she tried not to think about it. She couldn't answer her own question.

"I dunno, Steve," she said with sigh.

Steve looked at her. "*Eta-ruua unma eo sua, unhar-loa?*"

She grinned wryly. "I'm going to take it on good faith that's not an insult."

The door at the end of the corridor slid open and the science team walked in. Cass waved at her.

Elena and Steve looked at each other for a moment before she stood. Her replacement had arrived with the team. She was, though she didn't show it, disappointed she wouldn't be able to listen in on the session.

Cass caught her. "I actually have the day off—wanna get lunch?"

"Sure thing."

But before they headed off, Elena pulled a rather sulky looking Rhys aside. She could tell he was in a foul mood, his expression resembling a thundercloud, but he didn't snap at her, though it seemed he wanted to.

"Do you know what '*Eta-ruua unma eo sua, unhar-loa*' means?"

The clouds dissipated at the linguistic challenge,

and he thought for a moment. He plugged a few of the words into the DL.

"Well *sua* is 'you' and *eta-ruua* is something like 'no more' or 'nothing.' *Eo* is a question, probably 'what' or 'have.' And *unhar-loa* is a diminutive, I think, of *unhar*, 'warrior,' so probably 'little warrior.' My best guess is that he asked if you've run out of words, and called you little warrior."

The explanation almost made Elena smile as she put it into context, but she checked herself, knowing Rhys was watching her. His mouth opened to ask her why Steve had said such a thing, but Elena moved off with Cass following close behind.

Cass took up the torch.

"What was that about?"

"What was what?"

She made a face. "That phrase. Where'd you pick it up?"

"Oh, St—er, the native muttered it, and I wanted to make sure it was nothing bad."

"Mm hmm."

Cass didn't say anything more on it, quietly thinking to herself until they made it to the nearest restaurant. What passed for fine dining on Terra Nova was pretty much anything you could get at the sparsely stocked stores, but prepared for you. It was put in the ration book like everything else. The reason for going was that the restaurants were staffed by people who had some culinary background on Earth, so you could get artfully toasted bread with a sort of jam made from native berries. While simple, the thought of jam and bread made Elena's stomach rumble.

"So how's the native been doing?"

"Fine," Elena said, sitting down at an outdoor table.

"Has his mood changed at all?"

"No, still quiet. But I would be too if I were him."

Cass nodded, though her eyes were down on her reader.

"What're you taking notes? I thought you had the day off."

"What? Oh, no, I'm telling Hugh where we are."

"Oh."

Cass looked up. "You don't mind, do you?"

"Why would I mind?"

"Oh you know . . . "

Elena did know, though she wouldn't admit it. Over the past year it had become apparent, though he tried to hide it, that Hugh was beginning to have feelings for her. At least that's what Cass thought. Neither would embarrass him by calling him out, but Cass was still suspicious.

Though Elena thought Cass was being a bit dramatic, she couldn't help feeling there was a small truth to it. She caught Hugh looking at her sometimes, in *that* sort of way, and more than once he had asked her to be careful on missions. She knew this amounted to little in the way of evidence, but for Hugh, who she knew to be reserved, it was somewhat unusual behavior.

She began twisting a lock of black hair around her finger as she waited for Cass to finish typing.

"How's the translation coming?" she asked.

"Slower than we'd like," Cass admitted. "He isn't exactly chatty. Though it's really interesting how much he'll communicate with Rhys."

"That's because he hasn't gotten to know him yet."

Cass frowned. "What's that supposed to mean?"

"That Rhys's a pill," she said, resting her chin on her hand.

"He's not that bad," Cass argued. "You're just mad at him for Hugh's sake."

"He has a talent for getting in trouble, which makes work for me."

"He has a talent for languages. He's learning ridiculously quick. And he hasn't done anything in a long time."

"I'm not saying that he's a bad kid, not all the time," Elena said, sore that this rare time with

Cass was turning into an argument, "but what I *am* saying is that he can be a pill."

"You don't know everything that's happened to him."

"Do you?"

"You know as well as I do that something happened that night, to *both* of them. I'm just saying don't be too quick to judge."

"He was a pill before that."

Cass sighed and threw her hands up. "I don't want to argue about this. Let's talk about something else."

"Yes, please."

They sat in a painful silence.

It wasn't that Elena disliked Rhys—well, she didn't like him, not much at least, but what really lay at the heart of it was that she found him hard to read. She didn't like that. She knew who Cass and Hugh were. She knew who Sergeant White, her mentor, was. Hell, she even knew who General Hammond was. With Rhys it was different.

Maybe what made it difficult was that he looked so damned much like Hugh. Every time she saw him made her think of a younger Hugh, aboard the starship. She had known that boy very well—perhaps better than she knew the adult—but it wasn't Hugh standing in front of her.

It was more than that, though. Rhys always had the look about him like he was carrying a secret. He moved quietly, kept a low profile. He had a peculiar way of looking at you, Elena thought, like he was searching for something, trying to read your thoughts, while being guarded against any sort of reciprocation.

"There's Hugh," Cass said, breaking Elena's train of thought.

She was momentarily sorry that both of them were greeting Hugh with sour looks but found he had one to match.

Cass couldn't even get her mouth open to greet him before he demanded, "What's Rhys doing with the science department?"

This caught Cass off guard, and both of them looked at Hugh in surprise. His tone was low, almost a growl. He had never spoken to them like that.

Elena watched as Cass thought a moment and then frowned.

"He's doing what he thinks is right," Cass answered.

Hugh slammed his fist on the table, and Elena's instincts kicked in. She jumped up, her hand going to her hip. There was a pain in her gut and Elena, with hands that trembled ever so slightly, realized that her instinct was to pull a gun on Hugh. Her friend. The disgust threatened to overwhelm her.

"What's going on, Cass?" he bellowed, ignorant of Elena's turmoil. "Why's he working there? What're you making him do?"

"I can't tell you," she insisted.

That only made Hugh's eyes darken, like a storm cloud.

"It's not anything bad, I—"

He slammed his fist again.

"Hey!" Elena barked, shoving him. "Back off!"

He glared at her. "And what side are you on?"

"This isn't about sides you idiot!" she spat. "It's about why you're acting like an ass."

"So now you two are keeping his secrets. Great. Just great."

"Oh my god, Hugh, do you even hear yourself?" Elena said. "What's the matter with you?"

"You know our jobs make us keep secrets. Yours does too."

His eyes narrowed as he looked between them, trying to determine if they were truthful.

"What's going on?" Cass asked, her voice softening.

Even Elena could see that whatever was going on in Hugh's head had nothing to do with her or Cass. Hugh was quick to realize this too, and his face went from night to day. Well, a cloudy day.

Sinking into one of the seats, Hugh put his face in his hands and groaned.

"I don't . . . I'm sorry, I . . ."

Cass leaned close, quick to forgive. She put a gentle hand on his back. "What's wrong?"

He shook his head in his hands.

Elena, slower to forgive, sat back down and watched him. She had never seen anything like that from Hugh and it unnerved her.

"He won't tell me anything," escaped between Hugh's fingers. "I try not to worry, but . . . "

"He's just finding his own way," Cass crooned.

"I've just made a mess of things." He didn't seem very aware of them anymore. "Nothing's gone right, even from the beginning. I-I can't . . . I just can't."

Something in his voice shook her, pulled her out of herself. Elena reached out a hand and gripped his arm. Her vice grip forced him to look at her, not his breaking spirit.

"None of that," she said. "It's gonna be fine."

"I'm an idiot," he murmured.

"Yeah, but you're our idiot."

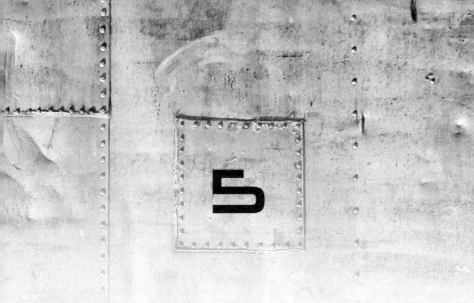

5

Rhys shivered even in the relative shelter of the prison and marveled at the thick skin of Charneki. It didn't bother the native—at least, he didn't show it. Granted, Rhys doubted he would.

"How are you feeling today?" he asked.

"*Muma ger nerma sua?*" translated the DL in a monotone voice.

Rhys grinned and looked up at the native. He was frowning down at the device, apparently anxious at the disembodied voice. The native muttered something under his breath and didn't reply.

"Not in the best mood I see," said Dr. Oswald as he came up the block.

He carried two cups of warm water with melting vitamin tabs. Rhys blew on the hot liquid when it was handed to him and savored the feeling of warm citrus running down his throat.

"He's barely talking to me anymore," Rhys said. "I think he's been here too long."

"Well we might be able to remedy that. Soon, anyway."

Rhys looked up, startled. "They're gonna let him out?"

Dr. Oswald's lips spread in a slow grin. "Better. They might be sending him home."

Rhys didn't know if he believed it and had a dubious expression to match.

"Why?"

"It seems the general's had a change of heart."

Rhys made a face.

"I know it sounds hard to believe, but she's been hearing a lot of talk from all sides that these skirmishes, if you will, with the natives are unpopular. She seems to be coming around."

He would believe it when he saw it, but Rhys kept that remark to himself.

"So she's letting him out?"

Dr. Oswald smiled with half of his mouth and leaned down to say, "It's only in the beginning stages of planning, but I have it on good authority that he's to be returned to his people."

"You mean someone's taking him to Karak?"

He nodded. "A whole team will be outfitted. We're hoping his return might foster a bit of good will."

"I don't think they'll like you getting close to their city."

"Probably as much as we don't like them getting close to ours."

Not knowing what to do with that, Rhys idly played with the DL. He knew the doctor's statement had a bit of truth in it, but he didn't like its tone. Rhys felt adamant about their new home being on land that was the Charneki's—the abandoned village to the south was proof enough of that. His sentiments weren't popular, however, not even with the more liberal science department.

Dr. Oswald cleared his throat. "We're hoping to establish some sort of relationship with the natives—a less violent one, that is. They must understand we're here to stay."

"And how're you going to make them 'understand'?'"

He checked his tone but knew a little of his disapproval came through.

"By diplomatic means," said the doctor after a moment. "We're hoping his safe return will necessitate peaceful conversation."

Rhys nodded. In truth he was only half paying attention, his mind consumed by a torn feeling. Part of him was happy to see the native returned to his people. It was wrong of them to keep him in the first place, especially in such an inadequate prison. Yet another part of him, one that he couldn't put his finger on, felt uneasy.

"I was hoping, Rhys, that you'd consider coming with us."

This snapped him back.

"What?"

Dr. Oswald smiled again. "We're going to need our best translator if we have any hope of gaining ground. You've been an enormous asset to this project. I'm heading the diplomatic expedition, and I've already personally asked General Hammond to let you accompany me."

Rhys's face didn't know what to do, caught between a smile and a wide-eyed stare.

Dr. Oswald stuck out his hand. "Well, what do you say?"

Rhys bit his lip, but only for a moment. Taking the doctor's hand, he said, "I'm in."

———

"They are planning something. They must be," said Zeneba to her council. "We must preempt them wherever possible. Our sabotage campaign has succeeded, but it is not enough."

"What more do you suggest, Golden One?" asked Chieftain Ura, the noble leader exiled from his tundra villages in the north.

"We must send them a message."

"Somehow I do not think they can read our script," remarked Elder Vasya.

Zeneba's lip twitched, but she ignored him and continued, "They have responded to us with force. It is clear that this can only be solved with similar means—it is all they understand. We must launch an attack of our own."

"What has happened to our peace-loving *mara*?" Elder Vasya asked. Zeneba half expected him to look around in a mock attempt to find her.

Her blood boiled. She bit her tongue to stop herself from replying.

The council was restless, shifting from foot to foot, muttering amongst one another. It was commonplace for Elder Vasya to question her. It was usual for these meetings to descend into argument. But all could tell, including Zeneba, that both the Elder and the *mara* were feeling especially irascible today.

Grinding her teeth, Zeneba persisted, "One strong wave of attack should send our message clearly, perhaps even weaken them sufficiently to make them think twice about pressing further south. This I feel will secure us through the winter."

"That would be ill-advised, Golden One."

Zeneba glared at Elder Vasya from the corner of her eye.

"Come then, Wise One, I would know your thoughts. If you have a better plan, then please, enlighten us."

"Anything would be better than a frontal assault."

She scoffed. "And here, only a cycle ago, you were preaching war. What has happened to the warmongering Elder?"

Hushed uneasiness enveloped the Red Hall. It

seemed most palpable to the sightless Elder Zhora, who placed a dry hand on hers.

"Please, Zeneba," he implored.

Elder Vasya turned to face her with his imperious frown, and she sat straight, ready for him. She removed her hand from Elder Zhora's, placing it in her lap.

"You cannot win against the demons," Elder Vasya said. "Not like that."

"I did not know you were a Brave One as well as a Wise One, Elder. You have been hiding your battle experience from me."

At this the Elder reacted as if she had slapped him, his head reeling back. He took the indignation with a wide open mouth. She held his astonished gaze, feeling sickeningly satisfied at the barb.

Something inside of her felt disgusted. It made her stomach clench and her tongue feel swollen. But she beat this down with a ferocity that almost scared her.

"How dare you?" came from the Elder's lips in a growl.

She faltered.

"I-I only wish to hear your advice, Wise One, regarding things you know something about."

He flushed into a deep, enraged crimson, and Zeneba felt herself sink into a startled blue. She had rarely ever seen an Elder any other color than a tranquil gold. This outburst of emotion from him shook her, and she almost cried out for Yaro.

"*I* have dedicated my life to the teachings of our people," he boomed, his voice echoing in the Hall. "Nothing has eluded my study. You, Golden One, have accomplished nothing."

She recoiled from the sting and almost lost her nerve, unable to take what she had so willingly given.

"You could raise an army greater than any Charnek has ever seen—you could call the Sunned Ones from Their heavenly Realm and have Nahara set her encrusted spear upon the demons—and still *you* would fail. You cannot lead them. You never could. It was foretold you would see the end of an age and so you shall. You bring nothing but ruin upon us."

Everyone in the Hall stood gaping, rendered speechless by the offense. It was an affront to Zeneba, to her seat, to the Sunned Ones themselves. Elder Vasya didn't look remorseful. He stood his ground, unmoving, scowling intently. His iridescent skin shimmered in his rage.

Worried he had not said all his peace, Zeneba asked with a voice lacking its former luster, "And who should lead us, then?"

Elder Vasya didn't condescend to reply, but his answer was clear from his displeased, downturned mouth.

"I see into your heart, Elder. You have acquired a taste for my seat," she said, though still much quieter than she wanted.

"What are you saying, Golden One?" asked an Elder.

"Do you accuse an Elder?" demanded another.

She gazed out at the turning council feeling like she had swallowed a rock.

"Elder Vasya has never supported my reign," she said. "Always he criticizes me. He questioned the Skywatcher's vision about Nahara choosing me. I accuse him no more than he accuses the Skywatcher."

"You do not know what you say," Elder Zhora insisted hastily. "You speak from a dark place. Please, *mara*, forgive him. Forgive him, and forgive yourself."

She stood, indignant, flushed red herself. The Skywatcher's words were too painful to face, so she turned from them, embracing instead the much easier anger that battered down her will and made her shimmer crimson.

"I know exactly what I say. Elder Vasya is a blasphemer."

There were gasps and cries from the council.

"You cannot say such things!"

"How dare you?"

"You speak out of turn!"

"*I* am *mara*!" she cried. "My word is Nahara's, and Nahara's is unquestionable!"

"To proclaim someone blasphemous is to banish them, and you cannot, Golden One, banish an Elder," said Elder Zhora.

"You are right, Skywatcher, she cannot banish me," said Elder Vasya, his voice a low, even rumble. It was unnerving. "But then, she would not know *our* ways. She is an impudent child, and it has never been more obvious than today. She does not deserve her seat."

"Perhaps not," she hissed, "but I'll be damned if I see you take it."

The Hall descended into an uncomfortable silence, with Zeneba and the Elder glaring at one another, and all the others looking between them. Zeneba's head throbbed and her chest ached. Her council had turned on her; she could feel it in the way they anxiously watched on. Even laymen like

Chieftain Ura understood the insult she had made against a body that existed even before Yalah.

She was stung by the shift. Since she had come to Karak, the Elders, except for Elder Vasya, had been benevolent and supportive. Never had she questioned their guidance or their loyalty. Yet to insult one was to insult all, and she now stared at a lonely abyss, unsure how to step back.

"I think it best you leave me now, Wise One, lest either of us say something else."

Elder Vasya turned stiffly after a moment and strode with long steps out of the Hall. All watched him go.

There were a few quiet questions about what was to be done with him, whether the *mara* would persist to see him a blasphemer?—to which she remained silent, thinking a reply would only worsen her situation.

Understanding that she would remain taciturn, the council followed in Elder Vasya's wake and left the Hall. Soon it was only Zeneba left, with Elder

Zhora sitting on her left and Ondra standing at her right.

The Elder stood creakily. He took an ancient sounding breath.

"Yours would not be a reign without trials—this I knew. You were to face what no others had, and if you are unprepared, we are to blame. I have never questioned Nahara. I still have hope you will lead us through. But more than this, I wish you believed it too."

He did not wait for a response, which was perhaps better, as Zeneba found her throat choked.

Her head slumped down into her hands as she listened to the quiet shuffling of the Skywatcher leaving the Hall. How was it he always knew? Of all those she had met, Elder Zhora most deserved his title of Wise One. But for his wisdom, Zeneba hated him.

No, not hate—she could never hate the Skywatcher. She felt repulsed at the momentary hatred, slick and slimy in her gut. It was gone as quickly as it had come, but it left a bitter aftertaste.

He was right. He always was. Yet she didn't want to believe him. To do what he asked was too much. There were moments when she had overcome, had actually seen herself as *mara*, but they were fleeting. Harder than ruling was believing in her ability to rule.

When she was sure the Skywatcher was gone, she leaned up and peered at Ondra.

"I'd have you do something for me."

"Anything."

"Follow Elder Vasya," she said as his eyes widened. "I want to know where he goes, what he does."

"I thought you weren't—"

"That's an order, Ondra."

He frowned at her stony face.

"This isn't like you," he said.

"How do you know what I'm like?"

He flushed red. "I suppose I don't."

With that he stepped off the dais and headed from the Hall.

As she watched his receding back, his footsteps echoing, she felt an overwhelming loneliness again. She opened her mouth to beg him to come back, but closed it. She doubted he would.

She sat on her hard seat alone, the silence making her ears ring. Her eyes crept upwards, following the back of the seat as it rose higher and higher, joining other attached pillars as they reached like branches for each other, creating a stone canopy.

She felt eyes, ancient eyes, watching her. They were the eyes of her predecessors, and they sat in judgment.

Feeling oppressed, like there wasn't enough air to breathe, Zeneba fled the Hall.

Ankha, her caretaker, was waiting on the other side of the threshold. Slipping her arms out of the jade gauntlets and the heavy chain over her head, she handed over the *lahn-nahar*. She also took off all her jewels and ornaments until she looked and felt quite plain.

"Thank you, Ankha," she said with a hollow voice.

She could feel Ankha's gaze following her as she made her way towards the western side of the palace. The evening sun was full and warm, one of the last long days before the northern ice-winds would come. She pulled her robe around her, feeling it was more a shroud today.

Touching the smooth, rounded surface of the head, Zeneba leaned down and pressed her mouth to that serene face. If she pretended, he was only asleep. If she pretended, his skin was warm under her hands.

Her hands trembled as she wrapped her arms around the slim jade shoulders. Hot tears ran down her face, spilling onto his. A vicious sob wracked her chest.

"How could you?" she cried. "How could you?"

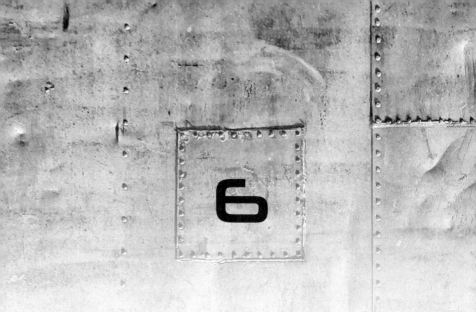

6

Elena arrived at the hangar with her pack slung across one shoulder. The hangar was already fairly populated with some military personnel working on the four speeders and three cruisers, while others collected baggage and loaded it. She recognized a few faces, but they were all from different units.

As she entered, she wondered about the patchwork quality of the delegation. There were people from everywhere, and the military personnel chosen didn't seem to have a rhyme or reason to them.

She herself had gotten the order only just that morning. *'Command No. 1127; Ames, Elena S.*

reassignment to Task Force Alpha, Unit 1, temp. Mission: Classified. Report to Hangar 2b, 11/36/2531, 0900,' it read, leaving more questions than answers.

Upon seeing her, a corporal with a reader walked up briskly and asked for her serial and name.

"Two-three-seven-nine-nine, Elena Ames."

The officer nodded. "All right, then. Your transfer is still pending, but it should go through any minute. In the meantime, baggage over there." He pointed at the small heap.

Elena was about to join the others and deposit her pack when someone called her name from the hangar door.

She turned to find Sgt. White striding towards them with a long, quick gait.

She put a hand on Elena's shoulder, saying, "I just got the dispatch. D'you—?"

"Excuse me, Sergeant, but this hangar is closed off. I'm going to have to ask you to leave."

Sgt. White looked the man up and down with

her signature withering glare, and Elena didn't know how he survived it.

"Well, *Corporal*," she said through her teeth, "her reassignment is pending, which means she's still officially with *my* platoon. I'd have a word with her."

The corporal was rather helpless as Sgt. White pulled Elena to the side. She made for a deserted corner and looked around anxiously, making Elena nervous. The corporal, now sulking, furtively watched them from a ways off, no doubt eagerly awaiting the official dispatch for Elena's reassignment.

"Is something wrong?" Elena asked.

She had never seen Sgt. White like this. Always calm and collected, there was a reason she was the head of the entire Vanguard Platoon. Instead the sergeant looked almost paranoid, with an uneasy glint in her eye.

"I'm not sure," she said in a whisper.

Elena waited.

"I want you to be careful out there," she said. "This expedition doesn't feel right to me."

"What d'you mean?"

"Look around," she said, nodding her head to the side, "barely anyone here is from the same place. Even those of the scientists were specially selected."

"Well this sounds like a specialized expedition. And how d'you know about the delegation?"

The sergeant gave her a look. "It's no big secret, Elena. And it's more than just assigning the best. I wouldn't insult you, or myself, by saying you're not the best. But there's *something* to these reassignments."

"What?"

Her forehead creased with a frown. "Is there anything you know of that'd get you assigned to this? Anything you might've done?"

Steve jumped into her head. She knew, in the back of her mind, that the prison, every inch of it, was under surveillance. For all she knew they had heard her conversations with Steve. Was that why she had been assigned? She swallowed hard.

"N-not that I can think of."

The sergeant heard her falter but said nothing. She looked around again then leaned in close, putting a hand on Elena's arm.

"Be careful. Don't give them a reason to send you anywhere else."

Elena nodded, and Sgt. White tried to give her an encouraging face.

"I'll see you when you get back, soldier."

With that Sgt. White took her leave, throwing the corporal another scathing stare.

Elena tried to look unaffected as she rejoined the delegation, though she had to wonder if anyone else was suspicious. The sergeant was the closest thing Elena had to a parent, and she didn't know why she should stop believing her now, but the alternative was something she couldn't stomach to think about.

"Ames," barked the corporal. "Your reassignment's come in. Report to Cruiser C."

Nodding, Elena headed over, dropped off her pack, and made to the cruiser. As she stood alongside, waiting for further orders, the official dispatch appeared on her gauntlet.

'*Reassignment, temp.: Confirmed. Task Force Alpha, Driver, Cruiser C Prisoner Transport.*'

Perfectly content with the assignment, Elena walked around the front of the cruiser.

"You the driver?"

Elena turned to see another officer's head poking around from the back.

"That's me."

"Great," he said. "You should start the preliminary checks. They'll be here soon with the native."

"Who will—?"

But the officer's head disappeared again. She didn't have time to think about what he said as a hush swept across the hangar, and Elena looked over. Through the door came a small party led by

Dr. Oswald and Rhys, and in the middle was Steve. His hands were crammed into full cuffs, and they looked as if they weighed down his slight frame. Everyone watched, unmoving, as the native was led to Elena's cruiser.

Few had seen Steve up close, and his presence caused obvious amazement. Though everyone knew what they were here to do, it was no less enthralling to be so close to an alien species. He strode in the middle of his human escort looking out of place. The way his shoulders were pinched told Elena he felt it too.

Steve looked at the vehicle with contempt, especially seeing the back chamber where he was to sit. Normally a cruiser could hold a dozen people, six on either side, in the back compartment, but as Steve was so tall with such long limbs, he would be sitting on the floor with only two guards.

After he stared at the cruiser, grimacing, for a long moment, the native looked down at Rhys. He said something to Steve quietly, in his language, and Steve nodded brusquely.

His lip twitching, Steve climbed into the back of the cruiser. His escorts smiled, relieved, and Dr. Oswald lightly clapped Rhys on the back.

From the group, Cass dislodged herself and went up to Elena.

"Just came to say goodbye," she said with a smile.

"How'd you get past the corporal?"

Cass grinned impishly. "I have temporary clearance. And I'm sneaky."

Elena gave her an eye roll. It would have to last her the while she would be gone.

"Why aren't you on this expedition?" she asked.

Cass shrugged, but her spirits notably dampened. "Someone's got to hold down the fort," she said, her disappointment not hidden by her chipper tone.

Elena put a hand on her shoulder. "I'll take lots of pictures."

Cass regained her grin and nodded.

"I'd better be off."

Elena let her throw her arms around her in a fierce hug.

"Don't get into too much trouble without me," she said.

"Same goes for you," said Elena.

With one last smile, Cass bounced back to Dr. Oswald, bade him and Rhys farewell, and then was from the hangar before the corporal even noticed her.

Feeling a little saddened now on top of suspicious, Elena walked to the back of the cruiser to see how everything was getting along. She poked her head around the hatch to find Steve making himself as comfortable as possible.

He looked up and saw her, and she thought he looked almost relieved, but that could have been wishful thinking on her part. They exchanged nods.

"You've been assigned, too?"

She looked down and found Rhys, his hands shoved in his pockets, standing beside her.

"Seems so."

They stood watching Steve get strapped in.

"You've done good work with him."

He looked up at her. His frown dissipated, and he decided to take the compliment.

"Thanks." He nodded at Steve. "He seems to trust you. Or at least . . . he's not suspicious of you."

Elena shrugged. "I'm only scary when I want to be."

His shoulders became pinched and his frown returned.

Elena realized only too late that he had been going for some sort of truce between them. As she thought about it, she was tired of mistrusting Rhys. Cass had been right, much as she hated to admit it, Rhys hadn't done anything mischievous in a long time, and with this new job, he had come alive. He was never late. He took pride in his work. If nothing else, Elena felt she had to respect that.

But then there was Hugh. She always felt the need to be mad at Rhys for him—he had certainly deserved it in the early days. Things were different now, she reasoned, and Rhys wasn't her brother.

She sighed and stuck out her hand. "Let's see this through, okay? No fighting. For him." She nodded at Steve.

Rhys was looking at the native as he took her hand. "Yeah, okay. Friends."

She almost opened her mouth to say she wasn't sure about that much, but she closed it in time. After he released her hand, Rhys seemed absorbed in his own thoughts, staring still at Steve. She realized, watching him, that Rhys was a lonely boy. In his determination to separate from Hugh, he had isolated himself. She saw in his face that when he looked at Steve, he was looking at what he thought was his only friend.

"Are you, uh . . . are you looking forward to going?" she asked, grimacing through her attempt at small talk.

"Definitely." His face was overcome with a grin. "He always used to talk about—" His eyes grew wide, and he cleared his throat. "I hear it's impressive."

Deciding not to question him, Elena nodded. "How'd Hugh take it?"

"Take what?"

"You doing this. I mean, you're pretty young."

"I'm old enough."

"You're like what, thirteen?"

"What does that have to do with anything?"

His tone was checked, not too forceful, but Elena felt he didn't like the conversation for the singular reason that he had had it already.

It was Elena's turn to clear her throat. "Well just . . . stick with me, okay?"

Rhys peered up at her from the corner of his eye. He shrugged. "If it'll make you feel better."

This trip was going to be the ultimate test of her patience.

"Rhys! *Rhys!* I don't care if I don't have clearance, that's my brother! Rhys!"

Everyone turned to find the source of the outburst. The corporal was putting himself between the rest of the hangar and Hugh.

"Dammit," Rhys muttered.

Elena rounded on him. *"You didn't tell him?"* she roared.

He couldn't answer through his wince.

Hugh was sidestepping the corporal by now, his eyes fixed on Rhys.

"It's all right, Corporal, let him through," said Dr. Oswald, who looked mildly interested in the drama playing out before him.

The put-upon corporal heaved a sigh and stepped out of the way.

Hugh made quickly to Rhys, not thanking the doctor. His fists were clenched, and Elena could see a jumble of words all trying to come out of his mouth at once.

"Where d'you get off leaving me *this?*" he demanded, thrusting his gauntlet under Rhys's nose.

She didn't have time to read all the note, but the gist was that Rhys had merely said he would be gone for a while. She rolled her eyes.

"I couldn't tell you everything," Rhys muttered, glaring at the ground, "it's classified."

"So you just up and leave without telling me anything or saying goodbye?"

Rhys cringed.

Dr. Oswald walked up quickly, saying, "This's a secret expedition—Hugh, wasn't it?—so don't blame Rhys. He wasn't at liberty to say anything."

"How long have you known?" asked Hugh, barely noticing the doctor.

Rhys shoved his hands in his pockets.

"*How long?*"

"A week."

Hugh threw his hands up in the air.

"And I'm only just hearing about this?"

Rhys finally looked up at him with a glare. "Well, it's not like you needed to know. *You're* not going."

Hugh's face came down in a dark frown. "Neither are you."

Rhys started like he had had cold water dumped on him.

"You can't—"

"Rhys is vital to the success of this expedition," Dr. Oswald said. "We need him."

Though he seemed to be trying to help, Elena noted that Dr. Oswald's words weren't soft. He had a steely look about him, and Elena didn't doubt that Rhys would be going with them.

"I'm his guardian," Hugh said, turning his frown on the doctor, "and I say he's staying. He's only thirteen."

The doctor pushed his glasses further up his nose. "I'm sorry to have to pull rank like this, but Rhys *is* coming. It's already been decided, and I'm afraid there's nothing you can do. Now say your goodbyes. This is a closed off area, and I must ask you to leave."

Elena watched Rhys throughout this speech.

His expression seemed to change with every word, from relieved, to surprised, to angry, to sorry. He was looking up at Hugh now with softer features.

Hugh took the doctor's speech gruffly, his scowl only worsening. He looked down at Rhys.

"It's going to be dangerous," he said, his voice losing its edge. "This isn't a game. People could get hurt."

Rhys hardened again. "I think I know that best of all."

Hugh took that as a final defeat and hung his head.

Angry at Rhys and even the doctor, Elena found herself putting a hand on Hugh's shoulder. He seemed startled, like he hadn't seen her there before.

"Hey," she said, her voice as soft as she could make it, "it'll be okay. I'll look out for him."

"Yeah?"

"Yeah. Promise. Nothing will happen to him."

He nodded. He suddenly seemed tired and deflated, barely meeting her gaze.

She took a handful of his jacket in her fist and gave him a small shake.

"It'll be okay."

He nodded again and finally looked at her. He put his hand over hers.

"Thank you," he said. "And be careful."

He tried smiling, but that was even sadder.

She wanted to say something else, something more, but she was lost. She had an overwhelming feeling in the pit of her stomach, but she didn't know what to name it or what to do with it.

With one last look at Rhys, Hugh turned and left.

The doctor clapped his hands together once Hugh had left, trying to revive everyone. He seemed far too enthusiastic.

"Nice going," Elena muttered to Rhys.

"He doesn't understand," he said.

"Neither do you."

7

Offering up the three plants he had gathered, Rhys watched excitedly as Yaro considered each of them quickly. Yaro's eyes flicked to his. He shook his head.

Rhys threw his hands, and the plants, up.

"You're never happy," he complained, '*Truar-ohnn sua-bua.*'

Yaro grunted at this. "*Khorrma nim pruan-bua.*"

Rhys paled at hearing they had all been poisonous and went out in search of something else Yaro might be able to eat.

While the Charneki didn't look emaciated, his cheekbones were a little too prominent for Rhys.

He hoped, when they stopped for a half-hour break, to find something he could actually eat. Human food didn't sit well with Yaro, not to mention that humans barely qualified their own food as edible. Yaro had developed a deep and not unreasonable hatred of the chalky substances forced on him. Compared to the native vegetation, Rhys could see why the nutritional supplements and protein packs didn't seem like food.

Rhys resumed his search, trying to remember what he had already offered. He had stumbled upon a native berry bush but hadn't had fingers enough to carry some, so he headed in that direction.

They had stopped that afternoon in a clearing after two days of dense trees. The going was slow, for even though they had been led to a Charneki road, it was narrow, meant for foot traffic not tires. They had had to fell several trees to make the path wide enough for the caravan of armored vehicles.

They had covered two-hundred and fifty miles

in three days, but what the regime thought would only be a four-day journey would turn into at least a week at their pace. The cruisers and speeders weren't suited for the terrain, especially the heavy vegetation, and everywhere they had to stop to clear the path, widen the path, or find the path again.

While the rest of the unit seemed rather put out, Rhys was having a marvelous time of it. The air was clean and crisp, the wildlife vibrant. It was everything his brown world back on Earth hadn't been. The untamed terrain was wide, open, green. Rhys wasn't the only one who felt overwhelmed by the pure wilderness—he often caught others gazing off into the distance, speechless at a sight no human had encountered in over two-hundred years.

As he plopped down on the ground to start collecting the orange berries, which had an almost sickeningly sweet fragrance, Rhys heard the back-up driver of his cruiser, Keith, talking to Elena.

"I think it's good we're doing this," he said.

"We'll see," Elena replied.

Rhys decided not to misinterpret her words. He always wanted to see Elena like other army dogs: mindless, brutish. But she made it hard. She seemed different. While she could bark orders and have the personality of a cactus, there was something soft in her, something that showed she thought for herself.

Yaro liked her. Well, 'liked' as much as he liked any human, Rhys supposed. He had doubts if Yaro even 'liked' him. At any rate, he didn't seem to mind Elena. Rhys wasn't sure if that was because he was used to her, as she was almost always the guard on duty while he and the doctor were there, or something else. It was mostly for Yaro's sake, then, that Rhys tried to see the better in Elena.

"Well it means we're trying to put things right," continued Keith. "And that has to be good for something."

"It'll be nice to see him home," Elena said, though very quietly, so that Rhys could barely hear.

"Exactly. We shouldn't have kept him in the first place, if you ask me."

Elena made a neutral noise and said little else.

Having collected enough berries—and hoping these wouldn't be *khorrma*—Rhys headed back to the cruiser. He hadn't found the conversation overly surprising. Many of the expedition held the same sentiment about bringing Yaro home, even the military personnel. It was nice to be around like-minded people for once.

Yaro sat on the back fender of the cruiser, just where he had left him. He watched Rhys approach, mildly amused by all the fuss.

Rhys held out his spoils.

"How about these?" he asked, '*Imm pruam?*'

Yaro extended his arms, linked at the wrist with cuffs—the smaller kind, which had thankfully replaced the heavy ones that confined his whole hands—and picked up a berry with one long finger and thumb. He gave it a sniff then popped it in his mouth.

"*Vanarr prua-bua irral. Ziia bua kalmah-na, lo an hatha-ui bua tomm-ni,*" he said in his rumbling voice. "*Io sua zai tuhrn malnaha-ni rua.*"

He grinned wryly, as if speaking from experience about the leaves (*tomm*) being bitter (*hatha*) and giving a bad stomach ache (*tuhrn-malnaha*), and Rhys smiled back.

Yaro took the rest of the berries (*kalmah*), though he seemed to be eating them more to humor Rhys than to sate his hunger. He left one *irral* berry in Rhys's hand and prompted him to try it.

Rhys knew he should be suspicious with the way Yaro was furtively watching him, but he lifted the berry to his mouth and mashed it between his teeth on the promise that it was *ziia*, 'good.' His face puckered almost immediately from the sharp sourness, and his eyes watered.

Yaro laughed heartily, his lipless mouth pulled over his teeth. Rhys would have laughed too if his face muscles could have relaxed. Rhys waved Yaro off, letting him have his fun.

The call came to resume stations. Keith came and motioned for Yaro to take his uncomfortable position on the floor.

Yaro's face lost all expression, and he gave Rhys only a nod.

"Aren't you going up?" Rhys asked Keith.

Rhys had spent the majority of the ride in the back, with Yaro and a guard.

Keith shook his head. "Nope. Your turn to be up front."

He meant well, giving Rhys a good-natured slap on the shoulder to move him towards the cab, and Rhys made sure to wear a grateful smile. In truth he had been avoiding being put in the cab with Elena, for he knew what was coming.

Seeing there was really no way out of it—at least no good excuse coming to him—he resigned himself to his fate and climbed up into the passenger seat.

Elena was already there, buckled in, making the engine rumble to life. She glanced at him as he adjusted his belt.

"Were those things actually edible?"

His gaze swung over to her to find a devilish grin.

He smirked. "Just barely."

The cruiser began rolling forward, the middle-most vehicle of the column.

The ride became smoother and the road promised easier travel. Curving away from the forest, it headed due south over rolling hills of grass and underbrush. Only another hundred-fifty miles to go.

Rhys liked this stretch of land the best so far, and he had loved the forests. Rolling hills of swaying green grass were littered with blue and white flowers, small crystalline creeks snaking between them. The caravan made their way up and down the hills, and as they crested, a soft breeze rolled through the open windows.

"So . . ." She glanced at him again.

His stomach clenched. Here it came.

"Why didn't you tell Hugh?"

"It was classified."

"That's not an answer."

He looked over at her. "What d'you want me to say?"

She gazed at him, perhaps a little too long given that she was driving. "To say you're sorry."

He could have laughed at the sheer simplicity of it, yet it struck him harder than he thought it could. If he was honest with himself, he was much less happy than he thought he would be. The trip was an adventure, and he relished being out in the wilderness. Yet he found no pleasure being away from Hugh like he thought he would. In fact, when he thought about, he actually rather . . .

He cleared his throat.

"Look, it's nice you're being a good friend. I get you were there when I wasn't, but—"

"Do you?"

She killed the words in his mouth, and he closed it quickly, a bemused frown on his face.

"As much as I can," he said. "And it isn't fair for you guys to always be telling us civilians how hard it was. We know it must've been rough—we get it. But we'll never be able to understand, okay? That's just how things are. I'm sorry you and Hugh had to go through that. Believe me, I'd have much rather . . . "

He cut away from his rant, worried he sounded too much like Ulysses Carter. He had attended several of Carter's rallies, had even seen him continue speaking while getting trucked off to prison.

The cab descended into silence and Rhys was determined to watch the scenery passing by. He wasn't in the mood to discuss these things with Elena, not to mention he felt she had little to no right to be sticking her nose in it. She wasn't his brother, and what was more, she wouldn't understand.

He couldn't help trying to peer at her from

the corner of his eye. She sat stonily silent, her gaze fixed on the terrain in front of them, but he couldn't help feeling that she was waiting, no doubt for that 'sorry.'

Rhys sighed. "Hugh and I just don't see things the same. We're on different sides."

"Sides?" she repeated. "What's this about sides?"

"Don't give me that," he said. "You know there's a line in the sand. There're those who support the war and those who don't."

"And you think Hugh supports the war?"

"Doesn't he?"

She gave him a hard look. "Hugh's about the least likely person I know who could hurt someone."

His jaw set. "Then you know him about as well as I do," he muttered.

"What?"

"Nothing. Besides, hurting others doesn't determine your side."

"What does then?"

He realized she was waiting for him to tell her what side he thought she was on. Knowing that was like walking through a field loaded with landmines, he steered clear.

"The regime tells him what to believe," he said. "They say the war is good, so he thinks it's good. He can't think for himself anymore."

Elena had been nodding vaguely along, but Rhys doubted she agreed with him.

"We won't get along until he starts thinking for himself," Rhys continued, suddenly feeling as if he needed to make up lost ground.

"And thinking for himself means what? Thinking what *you* think?"

He opened his mouth, reddened, frowned. "No."

"Mm hmm. So is it that you dislike him taking the regime's orders, or is it that you don't like that he's not taking yours?"

Rhys's mouth hung open, and he almost shook

with anger. He turned away from her gruffly in his seat, crossing his arms over his chest.

He knew from how much the question hurt that it rang with truth. His brain was having a hard time wrapping itself around the idea, but that didn't make it wrong. On Earth he had been the leader— he had taken care of them, had seen to Hugh. Now, on Terra Nova, he was the little brother.

The title made his insides twist. Hot tears brimmed in his eyes, but he refused to let them out. He couldn't bear the idea of crying in front of Elena.

His silence was proof of her being right, but he didn't dare open his mouth to contradict her. He let her have the small victory, if only to spare himself from worse truths.

———————

Not even the calm hum of the generators could pull Hugh out of his foul mood. Everything reminded him of how much Rhys wanted to get away from him, everything was proof that he had failed.

Hugh didn't know what to feel worse about. He entertained the thought that it wasn't entirely his fault, that he had tried his best, but that idea was snuffed out with ease, replaced with an overwhelming fear. Fear for Rhys, in the unexplored wilderness; fear of what would happen when he came back; fear that his brother was outgrowing him.

It hurt to know that for seven years he struggled with Rhys's absence; for seven years he tried unsuccessfully to fill the void Rhys left. Now, in a matter of moments, Rhys had tossed him aside without a second thought. He wouldn't miss him.

He realized he had been staring at the same wiring panel for a solid twenty minutes. All he could manage to do was rest his head on his hand as he continued tracing the wires with his eyes.

A slap on the back almost woke him. Saranov was squatting down beside him.

"What's the diagnosis?"

"They're fine," Hugh said on an outtake of breath.

Saranov looked over at him. He knew, perhaps even better than Hugh himself, Hugh's mind. He saw how it whirred and clicked. He knew how he suffered, how he hurt, but Saranov bore it all in silence. Nothing he had ever said or could say would make it better. So he put a calloused hand on Hugh's shoulder.

"Why don't you head home? It's the end of the shift. Get some sleep."

Hugh shook his head. "I'm not done."

"I'll finish up for you."

"It's fine. It's not like I'm . . . "

Saranov sighed. "All right then. I'm turning in."

"Okay."

He stood and stretched his back.

"Don't let me catch you in here when I get back."

Hugh nodded once, listening to Saranov's thumping footsteps as he walked away.

Hugh sighed himself, and his chest hurt. It was sore, and he could feel every rib as he drew in breath. He closed his eyes. Maybe it was better to turn in. He wasn't doing anything here.

Picking himself up, Hugh replaced the panel lid and tried working the kink out of his neck with the less dirty of his hands. Walking with his several tools over to the set of lockers on the other side of the long generator facility, Hugh replaced them and extracted his thick jacket.

There was nothing for it, Hugh reasoned. He wasn't going to change Rhys's mind by moping. Yet moping came so easy to him now. He sometimes worried that he would never be able to snap out of it.

Shoving his hands in his pockets, Hugh made for the exit. He heard voices not far on the other side, one of them Saranov's.

Hugh hesitated. It wasn't one of the other engineers he was speaking with.

" . . . And last we heard, they're a hundred miles out."

Thinking he recognized the voice as Colonel Klein's—General Hammond's second-in-command and an old friend of Saranov's—Hugh's ears perked up, in no small part because he spoke of the expedition. He hadn't been seen yet, so Hugh crouched down behind a work table, just able to see their faces if he craned his neck.

He knew there was something inherently wrong with him squatting there, hidden and eavesdropping, but an insatiable need to know that Rhys was all right overcame him.

Saranov nodded. "So they should reach the settlement in two days."

"Less if the terrain gets better."

"Does Headquarters anticipate everything will go smoothly?"

"That depends."

Saranov frowned. "On?"

Klein looked around for a moment before leaning in a little. "On which plan you mean."

Saranov looked incredulous and demanded explanation.

"This goes nowhere, Mika, you understand?" He waited for Saranov to nod. "It's top secret, but it's too ingenious not to tell."

Saranov frowned but waited for Klein to continue.

Hugh's stomach felt weighed down by ice.

Klein looked around again. "Headquarters wanted to ensure that the expedition would succeed no matter what, so we've implemented a fail-safe."

"How so?"

"The point of the delegation isn't to bring back the native—no, he's our ticket into the city."

Saranov's eyes widened. "They're infiltrating it?"

Klein nodded, grinning. "A good plan, no? If the negotiations go well, they'll hopefully be invited into the city. But honestly, we suspect they won't, and this is what the general hopes for."

"You *want* them to be taken prisoner?"

"Inside information is crucial," Klein reasoned. "Even if they're taken, accurate structural scans, population estimates, and more can be sent back to Headquarters. We have to know what we're dealing with."

"Why do you need all this?"

"Come on now, Mika. You know things will get worse. We need information we can use."

"And do you have any plans to get the delegation back? What's going to happen to them?"

Here Klein smiled. "That's the other ingenious part. The vehicles were outfitted to deal with any unfriendly situation. If they need to they can convert one into a bomb. We don't anticipate their being in any real danger—the natives are simple. On top of that, except for a few, we sent undesirables, ones who were making a mess of things for the colony. The few who know about the actual intention of the expedition will of course be recovered if possible."

"And you're just assuming the natives will be that good-natured? What if they're killed?"

Klein shrugged. "I can't think of a better publicity statement."

Saranov was quiet for a long moment, and Klein searched his face for some response.

"How could you, Anton?" Saranov murmured. "How could you do such a thing?"

Klein stiffened, his mouth becoming a thin line. "It needed to be done, Mika—for the good of the colony."

Hugh's entire body had gone cold, and his hands were trembling. The regime had sent them all into a trap. Rhys wasn't coming back; the natives would take him, kill him, and Hugh would never see him again. And Elena . . .

Something in him took over then. He had felt it only once before, when he got into a fight aboard ship with several older apprentices because they ganged up on Elena. It was a blind rage. He didn't think, just moved.

He only had a second. He dashed for the side door, crossing the light of the main entrance where Saranov stood with Klein. There was a shout as he pulled open the door and ran out into the cold night.

His feet pounded the hard ground, his hot breath making little clouds. He ran, ran for the hangar, only one thing on his mind. He had to get to them.

He tripped, picked himself up, kept running. There was noise behind him, a slamming door, a—

"NO!"

Three gunshots blasted through the cold air, and Hugh threw himself on the ground. Looking behind him, he saw, illuminated in the light of the facility door, Saranov struggling with Klein over a gun.

His blood pumping, Hugh scrambled up and ran. The hangar wasn't far—he could make it.

His irritation was unbearable as he waited for the guard to walk around the perimeter. He waited through two intervals, timed each. When the guard had disappeared around the other side of the hangar, Hugh ran to one of the side doors.

Numb, shaking fingers made the work slower. He tried to contain his hot agitation, resisting the urge to pull out all the wires. He tried to think, tried to make himself be precise. He traced one of the wires up into the command box and pulled it. There was a small buzzing and the door opened without trouble after a push.

The hangar was empty and dark. The vehicles were all neatly lined up.

He made the split second decision for a two-wheeled speeder. The cruisers were covered but more cumbersome, and he needed to get to them now.

Jumping on, he made quick work of hotwiring the speeder, having had to do maintenance on Elena's several times. The speeder purred underneath him.

He eased it forwards slowly, stopping just at the hangar door. Pulling the great doors open himself was hard work, but once he made a large enough slit, he dashed back to the speeder and rocketed out into the night.

There was shouting behind him again. An alarm was raised. He had only a few moments left.

He pushed full throttle towards the perimeter. He could see it, not far off—on either side it was pulsating blue, arming. There was one middle section, still translucent. He gunned it and closed his eyes.

He could hear the whir of the arming perimeter; in one second, maybe two, it would be electric. He clenched his jaw. One one-thousand, two one-thousand . . .

There was a *whoosh* which opened his eyes. Only dark, rocky terrain lay before him.

Not letting himself think about how close he had come to an electrifying end, Hugh swung the speeder southwest. Finding the heavy tracks of the caravan, he followed in their wake, hoping he wasn't too late.

8

The morning was quiet, and in another time, Zeneba might have found it peaceful. The *va'ana* were calling to each other in longing tones. They would be choosing their lifelong mates soon, building nests and raising young.

As Nahara rose, lonesome, into the pink sky, Zeneba found herself in one of the many splendid palace gardens. She had a fleeting wish that she had chosen a different one, for standing in this one was the tall, gleaming statue of Yalah. His eyes seemed to watch her as she wandered through the *viia* bushes.

She had a sudden feeling of remorse as she looked upon the statue. She had come here with Zaynab many times—she remembered how he jokingly made his face as stern as the statue. She pushed the remembrance down until it was stifled.

She momentarily welcomed the sound of shuffling feet, for it drew her out of the suffocating feeling that always came when she tried to smother her emotions.

Her feelings were quick to change as she beheld the Skywatcher ambling towards her with a slow, steady gate. He seemed determined.

"Good morning to you, Golden One."

"Good morning, Wise One."

Zeneba's desire to flee from him was overwhelming, but she kept herself rooted in place. Something inside her detested wanting to run from the Skywatcher. She had already treated him so poorly.

"A walk is a good idea, I think," he said. "The

ice-winds are coming, and soon there will be no flowers."

She wished he would get on with what she knew would be admonishment. She steeled herself for it.

"As your Head Councilor, I feel I must, *mara*, warn you about events that will come to pass."

"You've had a vision?"

He shook his head. "No, no. Nahara is quiet of late. She is watching."

"For what?"

His forehead creased in a small frown. "She waits to see what you do, Golden One."

Her chest felt leaden at this, and she was overcome with dizziness.

"Please, Zeneba, I did not come to speak of such things. The divine is mysterious and we cannot read into their will too much. What I wish to warn you about has much more temporal consequences."

Zeneba sighed. "You won't reconcile him to me, Skywatcher."

"Yes, I understand. There is nothing I can say to

change your mind. However, I will say this—Elder Vasya, by nature, has a fiery spirit. For many cycles I doubted he would be able to enter our order, for he was too willful. Yet he worked tirelessly on a tenacious self-control, one so strong I have not yet seen its rival."

Zeneba voiced her doubt, believing the Elder had exhibited no such restraint with her.

"Oh, it is quite the opposite, I assure you. His behavior of late is merely a shadow of what could come to pass. He is proud, something he was never able to purge himself of, and he will not be able to bear the accusations and insults you have laid against him. No, his very soul will revolt against them. He will not stand for it."

"What are you saying, Wise One?"

The Skywatcher took a long breath. "I fear these cycles have worn down his self-control. He has doubted you. That doubt has gone against all of our teachings, for if we believe nothing else, it is that Nahara is perfect in her discernment. He has met with failure again and again as you resist his advice, and this only became worse as you grew."

"Skywatcher, I—"

He held up a hand. "Please, let me finish. I am not criticizing, merely trying to illustrate for you where the Elder has come from and where he might go. These failures have, I believe, finally eaten away at that self-control he worked so keenly to build. Now, with your accusations, he will, I fear, completely rid himself of his learned constraints. He will not stand for such treatment, Zeneba. In spurning him you have made yourself a formidable enemy."

Zeneba set her jaw and refused to be frightened. As she tried to make sense of the warning, she reasoned too that there was little to be done about it now. He would not forgive her, and she would not seek his forgiveness. She resolved that if they were to be enemies now, at least there would be no more pretenses.

Besides, Elder Vasya had left. She hesitated to

tell Elder Zhora this, unsure if it had become general knowledge yet. Ondra told her of it two days ago, sullenly. He hadn't liked spying, thinking it below a Guard.

Where Elder Vasya was headed she couldn't say, and she wasn't willing to send Ondra to follow him.

The mountain bellowed. Her feet shook beneath her, and she reached out, helping to steady the Skywatcher.

"The horns . . . "

His words shook her almost as much as the mountain itself. Helping him to a stone seat in the sight of the entryway to the garden, Zeneba hastened from the flowers into the passageway, her pulse throbbing.

As she rounded the corner she collided with Ondra. Grasping her arms, he steadied them.

His eyes were alight and before she could ask, he said, "They've come."

"Who?"

"The demons. They're here, along the bluffs."

They ran, hand-in-hand.

"Are they armed? Are they here to declare war?"

"I'm not sure," he said, "but it looks like a small party."

They made for the eastern side of the palace, skidding to a stop along a colonnaded promenade. Karak stood in the center of a blue bay, flanked on both side by steep cliff-faces. To the south was the only sandy strip, on which stood the city of Oria, and to the north was the narrow opening of the bay, like a slice cut out of the stone wall.

Small figures moved atop the eastern bluff.

Zeneba clutched Ondra's hand. "What could they want?"

He was asking her what she would have him do, what her command was, but all she could hear was the sound of battle, the terrible noise their weapons made, and Zaynab's shallow breaths as he died in her arms.

"I don't want them here."

She murmured this, but Ondra heard.

"I'll lead a contingent—we'll flush them away from the city, out into the plains."

She was aware that she nodded, though what he suggested wasn't what she wanted. She didn't want him to go. He tried to move away, took her nod as approval, but she held fast to his hand.

Another warrior ran up to them, called for her.

"They have him, Golden One—they have Yaro!"

She went rigid. "Yaro? Are you sure?"

"Yes, Golden One. He is with them."

"H-how is he?"

The warrior faltered at her cracking voice, and Ondra put an arm around her.

"His hands are bound, but they do not seem to be threatening him. He stands with them on the bluff, out in the open."

She was nodding again, her mind in many different places. Overcome with the need to see Yaro, to know for herself that he was safe, Zeneba clutched at Ondra's shoulder.

"I'll go to them."

His eyes went wide, horrified. "No, Zeneba, you—"

"From what we understand from the Oria scouts, they seem to want to see you, Golden One," said the warrior. "They have not moved since coming, and it seems they mean to use Yaro to draw you out."

Ondra glared at the warrior for telling her this. "Damn what they want," he insisted. "You have to stay here. It's too dangerous!"

"Yaro would never hesitate to save me," she said.

"I'll bring them to you. Please, just let me lead them to the city. You can see Yaro then. I'll make sure, no matter what, we bring him back for you. But, Zeneba, you can't leave the city!"

Her mouth was open to tell him she was the one who was *mara*, that she could do what she liked and she wasn't to be ordered about, but all of a sudden the deeply rooted bitterness that kept such thoughts in her head snapped. She could feel it withering away, dying in her hot resolve to see Yaro.

She ground her teeth.

"Very well, then."

It took him a moment to realize she was assenting.

"Outfit yourself as strongly as you can, and take as many warriors as you can gather. Go there and find out what you can."

Ondra nodded quickly, anxious to be off before she changed her mind.

"Ondra!" she called, bringing him to a stop. "Bring him back. I don't care what you do with the demons—bring them, kill them, I don't care. Just make sure Yaro comes back with you."

———

They came in a tight, long column riding *garans*, a whole platoon of Charneki warriors. They were an awesome sight to behold, shimmering in the midday sun. With their mountain-city as a back-drop, Rhys understood how out of place the humans were there.

A murmur went through the delegation. The soldiers were uneasy, and Rhys caught Elena's hand twitching. He knew she wouldn't shoot, but it would have given her comfort to hold her gun, especially at the sight approaching them. The order to seem as docile as possible wasn't something the soldiers swallowed easily.

Rhys reached to his right and touched Yaro. Rhys tried to read his expression, but he was reserved. His mouth was a thin line.

"They've come for you," he said, '*Bura sua-na'a prua.*'

Yaro only nodded, his eyes slightly narrowed, as he watched the column approach. It seemed like he was looking for someone, and Rhys realized he was anxious.

"Has she come?" ('*Bura nua?*')

Yaro glanced at him from the corner of his eye but said nothing. His upper lip twitched.

Rhys could barely contain his excitement. He knew he should be worried—the column of warriors no doubt was supposed to frighten him—yet it was exactly like Zaynab described. A mountain-city in the middle of a bay! Cool, calm waters lapping up onto red stone, all leading up to a domed top.

He had thought—well, hoped, that she would come for Yaro. Rhys had the suspicion Yaro was close to Zaynab's sister. He didn't know why, and Yaro certainly wouldn't have said so. He had the feeling nonetheless.

From the looks of the column, the queen was absent. He thought he would know her when he saw her. Would she be waiting for them? Would she welcome them?

He knew the answer to that, yet he hoped. Perhaps, if he was allowed near, he could ask her about Zaynab, could apologize. He felt sure his pain was nothing compared to hers.

The humans were keeping to a tight defensive position, the vehicles having been carefully arranged in a semicircle. Several soldiers were behind open doors, watching wearily. Most of the scientists were still in the vehicles under orders. Everyone watched as the column came to a stop about twenty yards away.

The lead warrior, a gleaming red cuirass on his narrow chest, dismounted.

Yaro stood. He took a step forwards, but Rhys put a hand on his leg.

"Wait," he said, '*Quor.*'

Turning to his left, he asked Dr. Oswald, "Shouldn't we take the cuffs off?"

Without looking at him, the doctor replied, his mouth barely moving, "Not yet."

Rhys's face slammed down into a frown, his mouth slightly open in surprise. Why not? He couldn't voice his question, Dr. Oswald urging him on.

Rhys complied, returning to Yaro's side and

walking out with him and Elena. A few soldiers followed several steps behind. Something didn't feel right; his stomach was clenching, but he ignored it for now.

The lead warrior was young and tall, though not so tall as Yaro. As the older warrior approached, the younger's red hue slipped into a deep gold. Reaching out, he put a hand on Yaro's shoulder.

They exchanged quick words, not all of which Rhys caught, and the younger warrior sounded relieved. He was asking if Yaro was all right, and Yaro asked after the queen.

The young warrior touched the cuffs still encircling Yaro's wrists and made what Rhys guessed was a derogatory remark.

Yaro put his wrists in front of Rhys and looked down at him.

"I can't free you," he said, his eyes dropping, '*Hara-ohnn sua ya.*'

The young warrior, after a quick noise of surprise

at Rhys being able to speak Charneki, asked him hotly why not.

Rhys pointed at the small keyhole and shook his head. "I don't have it." ('*Eot rua vren-ohnn ya.*')

The young warrior snorted at this.

Rhys threw over his shoulder, "They want us to take the cuffs off."

"We want to see the queen," Dr. Oswald said. "Tell them we'll free him once we've seen her."

This deepened Rhys's frown. He and Elena exchanged a glance.

"We're not exactly in a position to negotiate," she muttered.

Hating himself a little, Rhys said, "*Mara.*" Both Yaro and the young warrior looked down at him with wide eyes. "We want to see the queen. When we do, we will free him." ('*Nik lahn mara lorrum ua. Vren dranar ua, lo hara due ua.*')

Both warriors flashed red. The young warrior cried they would do no such thing, and Yaro, in less words, denied them. The younger warrior, his eyes narrow and suspicious, said they wouldn't get near the queen, that it was an insult to think they would, but fell silent at Yaro's stony glare.

Rhys wetted his lips. "We do not want to fight," he insisted. "We want to be friends with the Charneki." ('*Nik lahn ma'an-ohnn ua. Nik lahn valya-bua ol Charneki ua.*')

The young warrior expressed his doubts with quick, harsh words.

"Ondra!" Yaro snapped. "*Immili!*"

He complied with Yaro's call for silence, his mouth clamping shut, but he didn't look happy about it and continued glaring at Rhys.

They conferred with each other, quickly and quietly, so that Rhys could barely keep up. The young warrior spoke through gritted teeth, and Yaro's shoulders were sharp and angled. He motioned with his head back at the humans, said more quick words.

The only thing Rhys could make out was that

the queen was the only one who could decide on such a proposal.

"What's going on? What're they saying?" Dr. Oswald called. His voice was tight.

Rhys waved him off.

The young warrior snorted gruffly and gave a sharp command over his shoulder. Immediately two of the warriors from the column sprang from their mounts and headed quickly for the city along the southern side of the bay.

"Where are they going?" Rhys asked Yaro, *'Humarr morrum prua?'*

"Lorrum lahn mara," Yaro said.

Rhys related that the warriors were off to see the queen. Dr. Oswald nodded, seemingly pleased.

"This could be going better," Elena muttered.

"Well what'd you expect them to do?"

She didn't reply to this.

Rhys couldn't blame her for her apprehension. They had known this wouldn't be easy—the natives had no reason to trust them. He felt sure the only reason they were not, at the moment, hostile was because they wanted to recover Yaro safely.

As they waited for the warriors to return with the queen's decision, Yaro and the young warrior conversed quietly. He didn't catch all of it; he was too absorbed in watching the warriors swim across the bay.

He did, however, believe they were talking about him and Elena. He caught Yaro make a small gesture towards him, heard himself called 'not so bad,' and he referred to Elena as the little warrior.

Elena recognized the word too. Rhys watched as the young Charneki warrior and Elena looked each other up and down.

"*Yaro, unhar dua-bua ummi sua?*" Rhys said, asking if the younger one was a warrior like Yaro.

Yaro nodded.

Rhys bowed his head to the young warrior, told him his name, then asked for his.

The young warrior remained silent, his eyes narrowed. His lip twitched.

"*Vanarr dua-bua* Ondra," said Yaro.

Rhys bowed his head again. "*Yan amar*, Ondra."

Still he didn't reply. He refused to say a word to Rhys while they waited.

Rhys, however, didn't give up. Despite the less than cordial welcome, he was anxious to speak with as many Charneki as possible. He was getting the language down pretty well he thought, but his pronunciation could use work. He itched to go to the city. Even from the bluffs overlooking the bay, the city was magnificent, nothing like he had ever seen.

"What's taking so long, Rhys?" Dr. Oswald called.

"It's not an easy decision," Rhys said. He was getting annoyed with the doctor's impatience, understandable as it might be.

"*Venna ninya'ma Karak muni sua, lo matya-ohnn vua sua. Venna matok mara sua, lo kutyan sua.*"

Rhys looked up at Yaro and assured him they wouldn't betray the Charneki and they certainly wouldn't threaten the queen. He swallowed hard at *kutyan*, knowing Yaro wasn't exaggerating that they would be killed if they tried to harm the queen.

"*Nik lahn valya-bua,*" he said again.

"*Hun sua. Boneer-ohnn tak prua-nim ya.*"

He understood Yaro's suspicion of the others, though he did take a little heart that Yaro might trust him at least.

Finally he saw the two warriors plying the water again. It was just the two of them, no sign of the queen.

Everyone watched in anxious silence as the warriors returned, bearing the news.

"*Buran lahn Karak prua,*" one reported. "*Lo zhen-ohnn honna-iriin ab ummal-iriin prua.*"

Rhys checked his beaming smile, and for a moment he was too excited to tell the rest that they would be allowed into Karak to see the queen, but they would have to leave their vehicles and weapons behind.

"We can't leave the weapons!" one of the soldiers said.

"I don't trust them that much," said another.

"It's a bad move," Elena told him quietly.
"What if—?"

"We'll be fine," Rhys assured her. "They won't
do anything if we don't."

Elena wasn't convinced.

"They will leave the mounts, but they want
their weapons," he told Yaro, '*Gamatn honna-ni
prua, lo nik ummal-iriin prua.*'

Ondra snorted, saying they surely weren't to be
trusted.

"*Bua mara a'val-irii rua,*" said Yaro sternly,
saying that it was the queen's will. He addressed
Rhys when he repeated it was the queen's will that
they come, and they mustn't defy her.

Turning back to the delegation, Rhys would see
what he could do.

"They'll let us see the queen, but not with our
weapons."

When the party still grumbled, he took a few steps towards the doctor.

"It's not unreasonable, considering."

Dr. Oswald didn't like it—his grim face was proof enough of that—but he sighed, relenting. Ordering the soldiers to stand down, all the guns were given to the four who would remain behind with the vehicles.

For a moment Rhys was going to remind them about their knives—he knew Elena had one strapped to the inside of her boot and who knew where else—but he decided that was a fight he would lose. No point losing barely won ground.

When the Charneki seemed satisfied that the humans were unarmed, the column, with a sharp command from Ondra, turned and headed down for the city along the bay. Yaro walked with Rhys and Elena, heading the small human party.

The walk through the city, which Yaro, after a little prodding, called Oria, was interesting though a bit uncomfortable. Eyes stared at them in amazement and terror from every doorway. No one seemed welcoming. The city stood silent, only the shuffling feet of the *garans* proving sound existed there.

Upon getting to the shores, there was a bit of a debacle procuring vessels to transport the humans. The sailors were unwilling to take them, though the warriors were even more so to let a human ride along with them. Finally, after three longboats had been rounded up, they set across the crystalline water.

He sat across from Elena and felt a little sad that she couldn't enjoy herself like him. Everything about her, from her taut shoulders, to her eyes flicking every which way, reminded him that she was on edge. He tried coaxing her into conversation, remarked on the astounding sights, but she wouldn't take the bait.

They were surrounded constantly by the warriors and their *garans*, the animals, while rather cumbersome on land, proving adept at amphibious maneuvers. Soon they were coming ashore along a set of wide, shallow steps, the first few of which were submerged.

Hopping out of the boat, Rhys and the other humans sloshed up onto the drier steps, awaiting instruction. The soldiers were uneasy, missing their weapons. Dr. Oswald looked rather green.

Yaro made a movement, indicating they had to start climbing.

The mountain looked smaller from up on the bluff, but now that they stood at the base, even Rhys paled.

It proved an arduous and unpleasant walk. The Charneki with their long legs didn't seem bothered by it and often had to slow, waiting for the humans to catch up or catch their breath. Ondra's annoyance was no secret, and often Rhys caught him muttering his wonderment at having feared them once.

Just like in Oria, the townsfolk of Karak came to see the spectacle. And that, Rhys realized, was what this was. By letting them come to her city, the queen was proving to the humans that the Charneki were powerful too, with cities full of people. She was also letting the Charneki get a good look at the humans. With how much they were panting, Rhys doubted they made an imposing impression.

Finally the great walls of the palace rose above them, adorned with tall, stately statues carved into the façade. Great gates of jade swung open at their approach.

Once inside, they started up a flight of wide, rounded steps that progressively narrowed until it reached the very top of the palace. Tiered walkways circled around to other parts of the palace, separated by bushes and flowers.

At the top of the red steps there was a wide, polished landing with balconies overlooking the city on either side. If they had had a moment, Rhys would have liked to take a look. Heady at the elevation, the humans did take a moment to rest, sucking in air and clutching their sides.

Before them stood a great archway, runes etched all around. Thick attached columns were carved into the outer wall.

From inside the chamber stepped an old looking Charneki clad in a turquoise robe. He had a white rune painted on his forehead. He observed the humans for a long moment, looking them up and down. After, he greeted them and said the queen was waiting.

Swallowing the lump in his throat, Rhys headed in first with Yaro and Ondra. It was an expansive room, the ceiling a high dome. There were attached columns inside too, all rising up, becoming branches and forming a stone canopy.

On the opposite side sat the queen. She was everything Rhys could have imagined. Tall, slender, regal. Her narrow body was outlined underneath billowing amber robes. Her arms were clad in jade and gold, and a heavy chain with a jade pendant hung from her thin neck. She watched them coming with what seemed mild interest. She was almost haughty, looking at the humans approaching her as if they were something she would find beneath her foot.

As the humans gathered before her, she glinted red, though, with a concentrated look, it faded into a maroon. Everyone was silent.

Finally, in a cold voice, she asked after Yaro.

"*Opiir lo ta'ana,*" he said.

Hearing that he was hungry but otherwise all right, she nodded. Rhys caught a spark of warmth in her eye as she continued to speak with him, her voice softening as she asked what the humans had done with him. It was checked feeling; she was careful about the turn of her head and angle of her shoulders, but he could nonetheless see she was anxious to know all Yaro's story.

When Yaro had summed up his time with the humans in his normal fashion—that being few words—the queen finally turned her attention to them.

"*Yan amar, mara,*" Rhys said, bowing his head. Several others had the tact to do the same.

Her hairless brow rose. "*Murre Charneki vanma dua?*"

He nodded quickly, grinned, replying that yes, he spoke a little Charneki, and he hoped to learn as much as he could. Yaro grimaced at his presumption.

Rhys's words had little effect on the queen. She continued looking on apathetically, although Rhys couldn't help feeling it was a ruse. Her eyes, though steely, were wide, searching. Her swirls of iridescent skin wouldn't stay one color, always shifting between shades of purple and red, even, for a flash, blue.

"*Ila vren li'ama sua?*" she said, asking what it was the humans were doing there.

Rhys repeated that they hoped they and the Charneki could be friends, *valya.*

At this she bared her teeth in a mocking laugh. "*Valya!*" she said. "*Nik lahn valya-iriim prua-bua?*"

Rhys, uneasiness suddenly making his insides squirm, tried to salvage the conversation. He assured her that yes, the humans wanted to be their friends.

The queen leaned forward in her throne suddenly, her skin losing almost all its color and turning white.

"*Kutya uin-ira sua, lo bra'aya valyian-ira?*" she hissed.

Rhys opened his mouth, tried to respond to her accusations. He hadn't understood everything, but all he needed was *uin*, 'brother.' In a flash he understood this was all for nothing.

She had worked herself into a hotly toned rant, and more accusations were thrown at the humans. He could barely catch any of it with Dr. Oswald demanding to know what she was saying in one ear and the queen berating him in the other.

"*Yual prua!*"

He didn't have to know what that meant. Warriors sprang from everywhere, surrounded the humans, and they were defenseless. Some soldiers scrambled for their hidden knives, but the Charneki, looming, dared them with their spears to try it.

"What're they doing?"

"Rhys, tell them we mean no harm!"

"*Yual lahn prar'ya-ni prua!*"

"What's happening?"

"Rhys, stick close to me."

"*Ta'eo lorra-ira mun prua.*"

9

The Hall buzzed like a horde of angry *uppas*. It was giving Zeneba a headache. She held one side of her face in a hand and watched as small factions of her council argued over what to do with the demons.

She could have laughed. All this arguing for nothing. She knew exactly what she was going to do with them. Still, she let them argue, found some small comfort in their turning on each other rather than her.

"They should be returned to their mounts and told to leave! We should not keep them a moment longer," insisted Elder Jeska.

"And seem weak?" scoffed Elder Ha.

"A few days in our dungeons and we just send them on their way sends the wrong message," said Chieftain Ura.

"They will go back and tell the rest how lenient we are!"

"If we keep them, the others will surely come for them. Would you risk more of them?"

"We should not have taken them in the first place!"

Registering the accusation, Zeneba lifted her head, though she couldn't quite shake the apathy that kept her face emotionless. She managed a small frown.

"That was not your decision," she said, "and neither is their fate."

This caused a hush, and she realized only too late that she had united them again.

"And what will be done with them, Golden One?"

"Yes, tell us your will."

Keeping her face cool, her color unchanged, she told them, "We will pay them the same courtesy they have us. They will be put to death as soon as possible."

As the words came rolling off her tongue, she almost choked. She had never sentenced anyone to death. She had had several cases brought before her in the past, had seen her share of criminals and vagrants. She had once sentenced a murderer to lifetime imprisonment.

But this was different. They were not Charneki, they were demons, and didn't deserve her sympathy or her mercy. She would do to them what they did to Zaynab. If they had had their way, he would have died alone in that frozen tundra. Through them she would send her own message.

Her words ignited a new debate and now there was shouting, echoing through the great dome. It renewed her headache.

"That is my will!" she cried. "I am in no mood for defiance."

This brought on an uneasy calm, and she could see in their eyes that they wondered if she would declare all of them blasphemers too. It made her chest ache.

Out of the corner of her eye she saw Yaro approach. He had resumed his rightful spot at her side, holding the great metal spear, as the Head of the Guard. She had hoped to feel a little more assured with him there, but the meeting had spiraled out of control again.

"You must not kill them, Golden One," he said, barely more than a whisper.

Enough heard. His words were passed down in hurried whispers through the rest of the Hall.

Zeneba looked on astonished. After just saying she was in no mood for this, Yaro of all people, loyal to a fault, was the first to speak against her!

Her face reflecting her darkening mood, she turned on him. "What did you say?"

"Please, Golden One, spare them."

Her hands clenched into fists in her lap. "Have

you forgotten what they did to Zaynab? You would defend *them*?"

Yaro's mouth inched downwards. "I remember, Golden One. I remember him every day. But I also remember a *maheen* I once brought to this city, long ago, and she was compassionate. She would say killing would accomplish nothing."

It was as if her chest had cracked open, and she almost checked to see if there was indeed a gaping hole. Her fists relaxed, began trembling. Her eyes widened, stung.

"He was right," Yaro said.

"W-what?"

"Zaynab. He said they were not all demons. He was right. Please, let me prove it to you. There are two, they . . . "

His words failed him, watching Zeneba's shifting color. It wouldn't fix, moving between blues and reds.

Steeped in dark blue, she said, "How can you ask me this? After what they did . . . "

"It was not these demons. Please, Golden One, meet these two. One of them has spoken of Zaynab."

She laughed, a single, harsh sound that echoed in the silent Hall. "And how do you know you do not bring his murderer before me?"

She could see the pain Yaro was in. He refused to meet her gaze.

"I would know if it was," he murmured.

With a quickness that startled her, she gave in. She could not bear to see Yaro pained so. She knew that she would do whatever he asked, for he was almost all she had left.

"Very well," she said. "Bring these two."

———

Elena popped the collar of her jacket, her cold cheeks melting into the warmth of the synthetic wool. She shoved her hands back under her arms. Her movements were stiff, her clothing not enough to ward off the cold of the mountain's innards.

If they hadn't had their gauntlets, they wouldn't have known they had been down there in the dungeons for two whole days now. There had been a small ration of food late yesterday, but the green paste was indigestible. Most of it had been vomited back up.

Dim, emaciated faces ranged around the long, narrow cell. All seventeen of them were packed in there, and there was no word when they would be released, if at all. Already there was grumbling that this had been a foolish idea.

In a few furtive moments of quiet, they had gotten into contact with the team left outside. It was hard to hear through the static, the mountain interfering with their signal. The team was being left alone for now, though there were warriors nearby. Elena knew that at a command, all of the vehicles could rain hell down on the city, enough hell that their release might become an option. Might.

Those who still held out hope, mainly Rhys and a few of the science team, refused this plan, at least for now.

Rhys was very quiet. She could see turbulent thoughts behind his pensive eyes, and she thought she knew the reason. Rhys had an idea of the natives, had thought this would go a certain way. Now that things had gone completely awry, he was disappointed, to say the least.

She nudged him with her elbow. His eyes flicked to her then back down.

"You okay?"

"Mm."

Taking what she could get, Elena left him alone. This was why she never let her expectations get too high. It was what made her a decent soldier. She was rarely disappointed.

Her head jerked to the cell door, the bars made of thick red stone, when she heard a high-pitched creaking. Soft footsteps descended into the dungeon.

She was the first to her feet, closest to the door. Her fingers itched to wrap around the hilt of her knife, but she waited.

She blinked, her eyes stinging at the blue light radiating from a lantern held over the heads of several natives. The burning cerulean cast dark shadows along their angular bodies. Through her squint she recognized Steve.

Rhys had jumped up at the sight of them, was pressing against the bars.

"*Oriim ala. Pretara ila-bua, Yaro?*" he said.

"*Bura lahn sua tra'ala ya. Murren lahn mara sua.*"

A relieved smile broke out over Rhys's face, and he told her, "We're going to see the queen again."

Elena didn't know why he was so excited. She was probably going to throw them off her mountain this time.

The native bearing the lantern made quick work of the lock, moving a circular stone panel in a sequence of rotations. There was a groan and the bars swung open an inch.

Elena turned around, frowning, at the sound of the bars shutting again. Only she and Rhys stood outside.

"What's the meaning of this?" Dr. Oswald demanded. "Rhys, ask them what's going on!"

"*Oma-ohnn prua?*" Rhys asked.

"*U'ana sua-ki.*"

Rhys swallowed. He and Elena exchanged looks. "She apparently only wants to see the two of us."

"Rhys, get us the hell out of here," said the doctor.

The humans called out, but it was a jumble of words with the natives giving orders. She fell in line behind Rhys as they headed back up the stone steps.

At the landing, she turned to Steve and said, "What's this about, Steve?"

She heard a small sound beside her and looked down, surprised at hearing Rhys laugh.

"What?"

"His name's Yaro."

She looked up at Yaro as they walked along an open-air corridor, the waning sun behind them. He looked more like a Steve.

"*Vanarr sua Steve nua,*" Rhys told the native with another laugh.

One side of Steve's mouth inched upwards, and he nodded.

Rhys continued chatting at Steve for the rest of the walk, and she felt at a keen disadvantage. She had a sudden wish she spoke their language.

She didn't have time to ask what they were saying, for they came to the big throne room. They were received with the same suspicious looks, though the queen seemed different. Her nostrils not up in the air, she watched them approach with tired eyes.

Steve conveyed them to her dais and stood beside them as the queen again looked them up and down.

"Oneer ohrn sua-bua Yaro. Gan'na dua-bua?"

"Mara, nim ua-bua ohnn zai. Nik lahn bua valya-iriis ua," Rhys said.

The queen thought a moment.

"Nik lahn ila mene lahn yua sua?"

"Uran op'ara Zaynab ya."

This startled the queen, her lipless mouth parting.

"What's she saying?" Elena whispered.

"She wants to know what we have to say."

"And what're you—?"

Reaching in his pocket, he extracted a small device and pressed it into her hand. It was the DL.

The queen said a few solemn words, and Rhys replied with equal feeling as Elena tried to figure out how to turn the DL on and then the volume down. They were having a soft conversation, as if no one else existed. It left Elena wondering what *Zaynab* meant.

Rhys's eyes had fallen to the ground, and the

queen had a distant look. Elena thought she looked sad.

"You make my decision hard," the queen said, Elena putting the DL to her ear just in time to hear the monotone translation of her words. "But I must lead my people, and your kind has killed many of us."

"You must do what you think is right, queen," Rhys said.

This seemed to strike the queen.

"You sure about this?"

Rhys glanced up at Elena. "She's in pain, not evil."

As he said this, the queen straightened, and she suddenly looked regal. Her bluish skin shimmered, settling into a beautiful purple.

"I cannot forgive what your kind has done to my people, but you will not die today. I will give you a final warning. Your companion will be sent back to your city with this message—leave Charnek, and I will set you and the rest free. If your kind stays, I will keep you forever. And if anymore Charneki are killed, for each that dies, I will kill one of yours. Do you understand this?"

Rhys's face sunk, and Elena's did too when the DL finished translating. They looked at each other.

They queen motioned at her. "Does she understand?"

"Yes, queen."

"She will leave immediately."

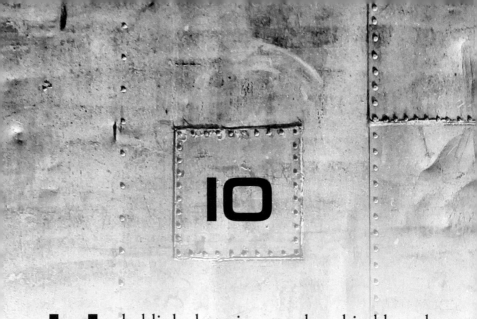

10

Hugh blinked, trying to clear his blurred vision. It did little, the darkened terrain all looking the same.

He could barely feel his hands or feet, the cold and his hunger making his whole body ache. In retrospect, heading off without prior planning, with no provisions, was a bad move. But he didn't think, or at least tried not to. All he could really think about was how hungry he was.

The three long gashes on his arm stung, cold gusts punching them as he raced along the tire tracks. He had tried to sleep the night before, thought he couldn't help anyone sleep-deprived.

Something attacked him in the small hours of the morning. He barely saw, just teeth and claws and scales.

Just fifty miles to go. He could do it, he could make it. He wasn't sure how much time he had left, if any. They had left five days ahead of him, but when they reached the city he wasn't sure. He was making better time; that he knew.

His determination to get to Rhys and Elena steeled him against the cold, though the wind cut through his layers.

He blinked furiously, his eyes easing shut. He nearly veered off the path. Refusing to stop, he revved the engine, pressed on. Three days of no sleep or food and little water had made him lightheaded, weakened. He didn't care. It didn't matter what happened to him—he just needed to get there, to warn them.

There were four tire tracks. No, that wasn't right. He frowned, blinked.

He felt his hand slip. Saw black. The speeder quieted to a hum. He hit the ground.

The night sky swam above him, small swirling lights dancing in a black void. His ears rang, his head ached. He couldn't move.

He closed his eyes, his limbs feeling impossibly heavy. He had to get up, had to go. He couldn't afford to waste any time.

His body didn't comply, and he lay there for what seemed an endless stretch. He faded in and out of consciousness, all the while feeling that if he couldn't get to them, he might as well be eaten.

Hugh didn't know how long he lay there on the cold ground. It could have been minutes or days before he was aware of something standing over him. Opening his eyes, he saw a figure. It didn't seem scaly.

Suddenly there were hands on him, lifting him up, patting his face.

"Wake up! Hugh, you gotta wake up! Don't do this to me!"

Startled by the familiar voice, Hugh's eyes snapped into focus.

"Elena!"

"Don't scare me like that!"

She had him wrapped up in her arms, and he threw his around her in fierce relief.

"What're you doing here?" she demanded.

"L-looking for you," he said, his voice hoarse, his tongue feeling two sizes too big. "I . . . it's a-a trap."

"What're you talking about?"

There were some shouts from over Elena's shoulder. He filled his fist with her jacket.

"Wh-where's Rhys? I-is he here?"

He tried to get up, move his leaden limbs, but Elena held him in place.

"Hugh, listen to me."

He stopped at her tone and looked up, his gut clenching, into her face. Her brows were drawn low, her mouth slightly open but silent, as if she struggled to say what she wanted to.

"Elena . . . ?"

"They have him, Hugh. Back there."

"Back . . ." He looked over her shoulder.

"No, not . . . Th-they kept him. The natives. He's being kept with most of the others back at the city."

"What?"

With pained eyes she related the native queen's message. As she spoke, Hugh felt himself losing feeling in everything. By the time she finished, he had gone cold.

"Hugh?"

She searched his face.

"I . . . I've lost him."